The Way It Is Now

Also by Sallie Bingham

After Such Knowledge

The Touching Hand

The Way It Is Now

STORIES BY

SALLIE BINGHAM

NEW YORK / *The Viking Press*

95001

CONTENTS

The Way It Is Now

AUGUST NINTH AT NATURAL BRIDGE

It was the habit in that family to celebrate birthdays—all birthdays, the parents' as well as the children's —not with parties and paper hats and the bounty of friends, but with expeditions. For all of them, it was easier. To have invited friends to the house would have been embarrassing for the children; no one they knew could have avoided staring, or drinking out of the finger bowls. Their parents had many friends, but they were the same people who had posed beside them in their wedding photograph, and it seemed tactless to acknowledge the years which had passed since that first occasion, years which had disfigured everyone except the central characters.

Each of the children was allowed to choose the historic shrine or state park where he would spend his birthday. The list of possibilities within a day's drive, although not long, was surprisingly varied. There were the limestone caves, Horse, Floyd Collins, and the Blue Grotto, which were patronized for the most part by ten-year-old Tom, who liked melodrama and fakery and admired the milk-white body of Floyd Collins, displayed in a glass coffin in the cave that had killed him. Then there was the marriage cabin of Abraham Lincoln's parents, which none of them cared for any more—tourists and school groups had begun to go there—and, farther east, the new federal lake and the park at Cumberland Gap. These were equally favored by Shelby, the youngest, who had remarked on his first visit to the concrete Roman powerhouse at the lake, "If this isn't beautiful, nothing is." Finally there were the horse farms, foreign-owned, corrupt, and flourishing, which Vivian had chosen for the last three years because they were only an hour's drive from home, which meant there was no excuse to spend the night.

The children chose independently, even unpredictably, according to the yearly change in their characters; but their parents, who for reasons of emotional economy only celebrated one of the two birthdays between them, always went on August ninth to Natural Bridge. By the time Vivian was sixteen, they had been to the bridge twelve times, and each time the drive up into the hills was the same, the Singing Pines Guest Lodge was the same; even the numbers of their rooms, which they carried around all weekend on keys jangling in their pockets, were never changed. The manager of the lodge had no trouble remembering how the Lysons wanted things done, but sometimes a new waitress, bringing in the cake with the single candle, would ask whether it was Mr. or Mrs. celebrating this time.

There was no reason to be afraid, and yet Vivian had been afraid for three years of the trip, as though each time she exposed more of herself by submitting to the routine. Yet it did not occur to her to find a reason for not going; her father would have been hurt, and she could never have stood that. He had a way of looking at her with silent reproach and despair which prevented her from acting on most of her impulses; he clearly knew what was best and besides, he adored her. (Her mother had used that word for it once when Vivian had not been expected to be listening. She had been embarrassed, yet ravished by the appropriateness of the choice, and she had used it after that to herself: adore, adoring. She could not quite believe, however, in the adjective, at least in terms of herself.)

Finally her mother tried to excuse her. "I don't expect you'll feel like going, this time," she said. "You must be sick of that place after all these years, and someday (your father won't recognize it) we are going to have to break the habit."

"You know I wouldn't miss the trip for anything," Vivian said sparsely. Her mother's attempts to spare her made her angry. After all, it was her life, the only life she had ever known, for she hardly counted her nightly forays into foreign territory. She was in love, and given to committing treacheries between eight o'clock and her father's midnight curfew. Still, that could hardly be called an alternative.

On the day of the expedition, the dew had dried by eight o'clock and the katydids were churning by nine. Vivian's father read out the forecast—"a sweater"—with satisfaction. The more difficulties, the merrier; they would take two thermoses of lemonade. He told the boys to wear shorts, and he would have advised Vivian as well if she had not already gone upstairs to put on a pair of stockings. The stockings were new and they had her name tapes at the tops to distinguish them from her mother's.

After she had dressed, Vivian closed herself in the back-hall closet and telephoned Steve. The clatter of the office behind him bothered her; his life would go on agreeably enough while she was drawn up slowly into the hills. At the end, she said, "I love you," and he said, "Have a good time," although she had never had a good time or even known what it was until he came into her life. She hung up the telephone and went down to the kitchen, where her mother was putting fried chicken into a wicker basket. "You can still bow out if you want to," her mother said.

Before Vivian could answer, her father came in. "Are you ready?" he asked, giving Vivian the quick checking look he gave her every morning when, to discourage suspicion, she crawled out of bed and went in her blue robe to have breakfast with the family. "Darling, you'll be fine as soon as you get that first cool breath of mountain air," he added and kissed her, gentler than her mother, younger and fresher-smelling too, with the lemon lotion on his neck.

"Daddy, what do you mean, smelling so cool," she said, and tried to catch his reflection in the tin sandwich box.

"That's enough, Miss," her mother said, whisking wax papers. It was ten minutes past the hour their father had set when they drove away from the house. The two boys were in the back seat and Vivian was alone in the middle. In front, Mrs. Lyson began to clean out her purse, wiping a film of powder off her compact and cigarette case. Mr. Lyson drove earnestly, his shoulders bridging the view. Vivian had to look across him to see the road, which passed at a certain distance from Steve's house. To miss a Saturday night with Steve and in the course to drive with her parents so close to his house—that was an abuse of her willingness to come and go in other people's cars, according to their wishes. Vivian was glad to work up a little indignation. Her face, in the rear-view mirror, looked as bland as lard. She craned to see Steve's chimney but lost it in the trees. His room was on the ground floor with its own entrance, and whatever his parents suspected, they never interfered; his mother looked at Vivian shyly when they met in the kitchen late at night. In the front seat, Vivian's mother turned her head as though she, too, were looking for the house, and Vivian stared at her neck, prodding her to say, "So that's where you go all the time when you say you're at the movies."

In the back seat, Shelby began his singsong for ice cream. His father ignored him, while his mother scolded, "Ice cream at nine o'clock in the morning!" Knowing how it would end, Vivian began to look around for a Humpty Dumpty.

Her father saw it first and swerved in across a line of traffic. Without a word, he jumped out of the car and went up to the ice-cream window. The boys were busily deciding what flavors they wanted when he came back with five vanilla cones. "I can't get something different for everybody," he explained, getting into the car and handling the ice cream back. Then he settled down to eat his own. Mrs. Lyson wrapped hers in a handkerchief and proceeded daintily, her tongue as pink and pointed as a cat's. But Vivian felt suddenly carsick and slid her cone out of the window. It would have passed unnoticed except for Shelby, who began to complain about the waste. Mr. Lyson turned all the way around to stare at Vivian. "Are you all right?" he asked with a frown.

"Yes, I'm all right. Of course I'm all right!" she exclaimed, and wondered if she were going to be able to survive.

Before long, the open fields began to give way to patches of wood, and on the rim of the smoky sky, the first hills stood up. They passed a sign that read, "Welcome! Blue Ridge Parkway," and their father ordered the windows to be rolled down. Mrs. Lyson had fallen asleep; she put her hand up to hold her hair but she did not open her eyes. She did not even stir when the car began to halt, hitch, and plunge from one possible picnic site to the next while the boys hung out of the back window to jeer at the traffic honking and stalling behind them.

"There's the place!" Shelby shouted, pointing to a public picnic table, and Vivian wondered why her father put up with suggestions. The just systems according to which the family was run produced in him a fury of self-righteousness, yet in the end it was always he who decided. Vivian sometimes heard him announcing these decisions to her mother: Shelby needs a summer at camp to take that fat off, Tom should learn to talk more, Vivian is old enough to look a little older. Steve never had any conclusions to offer, and when Vivian asked him why he was doing or saying this or that, he stared at her as though she had become, before his eyes, some kind of furiously functioning machine. "This is where we are going to stop and I don't want to hear another word," her father announced as he swerved off the highway and parked beside what was surely the ugliest view in the last ten miles: a heap of gravel and, downhill, a souvenir stand. Mrs. Lyson woke up and reached for the picnic basket.

Half an hour later, she was still chanting, "Chicken leg? Hard-boiled egg?" although they had eaten all they could, sitting in the noonday sun while the grass around them bent in the queasy wind from passing cars. The boys blamed the place on their father and he grew grave and refused to eat until Vivian handed him a chicken thigh. He looked at her gratefully and proceeded to devour the thigh and a breast as well. Afterward, he took the boys down to the souvenir stand, warning them beforehand that there was no money for buying.

Mrs. Lyson spread a newspaper on the gravel heap and sat down for the first time, stretching out her short legs. "This heat reminds me of the summer I was carrying Tom," she said and waited for Vivian to show some interest, but Vivian went on staring steadfastly down the hill. Her mother continued anyway. "I was sick as a dog every morning from January to June, never missed a day, and then that friend of your father's, Billy Lanaham, had the nerve to say, "I never saw you looking so beautiful.' "

"I guess he was trying to be nice."

Mrs. Lyson sighed. "I know you think I'm terrible; you're at the age when everything about sex is supposed to be beautiful. I suppose the race wouldn't continue otherwise. Here, don't let those sandwich papers blow everywhere."

Vivian chased one and brought it back. "I don't see what there is here to spoil. Daddy always chooses the ugliest place."

But her mother said sharply, "Your father has had a long drive," and Vivian knew her mother had used up her stock of disloyalty on the remark about Mr. Lanaham. Angered, she threw the picnic basket into the car. "Temper!" her mother cried in the trim way that killed love. Vivian was relieved to see the boys running back up the hill. They had bought a plaster figure of a child on a toilet, inscribed, "The Best View in the Blue Ridge." Mr. Lyson had only to look at it to laugh.

An hour later, they drove up to the Singing Pines Guest Lodge, and the boys cranked open the back window and dropped out. Vivian remembered years back when she had led the exodus through the back window. Now, halfway between the banderlog troop of her brothers and her parents' stately march, she walked toward the lodge, pulling her damp skirt away from the backs of her legs.

Through wide plate-glass windows, the afternoon sun was scorching the daisies on the lobby chairs. In one corner, a leatherette bench burned red as a coal. The electric fire was turned on in the fieldstone fireplace in spite of the heat; promotion for the lodge stressed the cool mountain air.

Behind miniature wooden privies and Vermont maple syrup, Mr. Lewis, the manager, was bobbing his greetings. When Vivian took his hand, he breathed out his "Long time no see" with the stale, irreproachable smell of pine mouthwash, which had frightened her since she was a child. Mr. Lewis smelled eternal, like the grave.

"Hello," Vivian said and blushed, suddenly aware of every physical change she had accomplished since their last visit. Mr. Lewis seemed to be measuring the thickness of her bare arms. Actually he had turned his attention to her parents and was asking the questions about health and enjoyment which Mr. Lyson loved to parry. "As well as can be expected for a man my age," he said, which caused the manager to throw up his hands and Mrs. Lyson to smile. Meanwhile the boys had gone to the windows and were exclaiming in false voices, "Isn't it beautiful!" They were not mocking; they had borrowed as best they could grown-up ways of admiring. Vivian looked out the windows once. Beyond the boxes of false flowers, nothing had changed. The pine forest, browning in the sun, lay like a mangy hide over the hills, and higher up, Natural Bridge, a lump of stone, hung suspended in the glare.

"She is too old to share a room with two great boys," Mrs. Lyson was droning behind her.

Vivian turned around quickly. "Mother, you know I don't mind. I can always undress in the bathroom."

Her mother looked at her curiously and then turned back to insist, "No, it just won't do." Behind her Mr. Lewis was rubbing his hands with embarrassment.

"But we've always had the same rooms," Mr. Lyson said gloomily.

"Times change." His wife was signaling with her eyes.

Vivian said, "Mother, will you please stop?" But her mother's chin had begun to tremble, and Vivian was given her own room.

The change ruined the day, dislocated their expectations: Vivian had a number on her key that no one had ever held before. They all trailed along to see her room, and Vivian was mortified at the sight of the great sacrificial double bed. The boys said it was beautiful.

"Everyone put on a bathing suit, we're going down to the lake," her father announced hollowly, as though over a megaphone. The boys streamed hooting out of Vivian's room, and Mrs. Lyson, with a submerged sigh, went to get her bathing cap, her towel, and her sun-tan lotion, useless precautions against the heat and the mud of the man-made pond.

"I'm not going," Vivian said suddenly, fixing her eyes on her mother's back.

Her father stared. "But you must be hot, after that drive."

"I'm more tired than hot, and I never have liked that mud-hole," Vivian said recklessly, taking off her scarf and shaking out her hair.

Her father was struck to the heart. "You always said you loved the lake."

Mrs. Lyson had turned around and was once again signaling to her husband with her eyes. "I expect Vivian has a good reason," she said.

"It's not the reason you think it is," Vivian exclaimed. Her mother often called upon their common female frailty.

Mr. Lyson looked perplexed. "Well, of course if that's it—"

"I'll be down as soon as I put my suit on," Vivian told him.

Her father came close and took her elbows in his hands. "What's bothering you, honey? You don't seem yourself."

His grip was deceptively gentle, and Vivian knew better than to pull back. He had held her by the hand, the elbow, or the shoulder ever since she was old enough to think about getting away. "Let go of me, Daddy," she pleaded, her arms limp in his grasp.

"You've been upset since the first of the summer. What's happening?" he asked.

"It's just that boy," Mrs. Lyson said harshly.

Mr. Lyson did not hear. Placing his hand on the back of Vivian's neck, he pressed her head down onto his shoulder; barely pressed, for her neck bent easily. He smelled as he always smelled of lemon lotion and dry-cleaned seersucker, and Vivian found herself shedding two luxuriant tears on his lapel, tears for the unkind way she had been treated that summer, for Steve's rude forcing and the shame and the soreness of her giving-in. Her father patted her neck between hot folds of hair. "Now listen, I don't want you to worry." Mrs. Lyson went silently out of the room.

"It's so hard, Daddy!" Vivian sobbed.

"It's a hard time of life," he said, and took her off his shoulder. "Now you get into your suit and come on down. You'll feel better as soon as you get into the water."

When he had gone, Vivian changed into her black bathing suit. She stood in front of the mirror to pin up her hair and stretched her elbows up like wings. Her small breasts rose smoothly under the black elastic and she could not help admiring them, as well as her bird-thin legs. She had a boy's body still, without an extra inch of flesh, except for the frills. The memory of her mother's legs, laced with thick blue veins, disgusted her as though it was her mother's fault that she had become ugly and old.

She went down the hall and knocked on her parents' door but they had already gone; her mother had insisted on that, Vivian felt sure, to give her a last chance to withdraw. She went outside and hurried down the concrete path to the lake.

The pond lay at the bottom of the valley and evening shadows had already stretched halfway across it. In front of the changing house, white sand had been spread on the mud, and her family were lying there in a close huddle. Beyond them, a band of local boys lay shoulder to shoulder; Vivian could tell they were locals because they were wearing tight, bright-colored sateen trunks. They lifted their heads to stare at her as she minced down the steps, and she drew her towel more tightly around her shoulders.

Her father had also looked up. "Isn't that a new suit?" he called when she was still some distance away.

"I got it last week."

Her father stood up and stretched, lean and elegant in his

short white trunks. "Last one in is a dirty monkey," he shouted
and sprinted down the beach. Vivian watched him fall full-
length into the water, casting up a curl of spray.

"Vivian's it," the boys shouted, running after him. Vivian
folded herself neatly onto a towel.

Her mother seemed to be asleep. Now and then, however,
her eyelids quivered a little. She lay in a heap with her knees
drawn up, as though she had been struck down.

"Next year I'm going to arrange for you to spend the weekend with Aunt Pat," she said without opening her eyes.

"I don't know why you should do that. I enjoy this, in a
way."

"I'm not thinking about you. Your brothers need some attention and they never get any when you're around."

"That's not my fault."

"Nobody's talking about fault. I thought you were so crazy
about that boy with braces on his teeth. I thought you didn't
want to miss a Saturday night with him." Her eyes were still
closed and the lids quivered rhythmically.

Vivian stood up, and at once the stranger boys lifted their
heads. "I'm going swimming," she said coldly. Her mother was
always hurrying her, pushing her out of the way, as though
she prevented something from being accomplished or enjoyed.
She stalked self-consciously down to the water, sucking in her
stomach and holding her breasts high. The boys' stares hung
from her shoulders like a train.

The water was warm and thick and gravy-colored; she waded
in to her knees, then bent and splashed herself. Her brothers
and her father were already swimming out to the raft, and
after a minute she slid into the water and began to backstroke
after them. As she swam, she heard splashing behind her and
knew the stranger boys had come in.

Lingering along toward the raft, she almost allowed them
to catch up with her. There were three of them; their round
heads bobbed in her wake. Mountain boys, they hardly knew
how to swim, and they thrashed the water vigorously and then
stopped to gasp for breath. Vivian floated on her back and

watched them. They did not exist for her except as mirroring eyes. Behind, her brothers were calling from the raft, and she turned over at last and began to swim slowly toward them.

Her father reached down and pulled her up onto the raft. "Better late than never," he said grimly.

Vivian did not answer. She stretched out on her back and closed her eyes, listening to the rippling water. The stranger boys were still swimming toward the raft, but they stopped a few yards off and began to duck each other. Their gruff shouts made her smile.

Her father sat down beside her, showering her face with drops. He was watching her brothers absently as they took turns diving into the water. "All right, that's enough," he said after a while, and Vivian was surprised to hear how slack his voice had become. "We're going in, it's getting late," he told her.

Vivian opened her eyes and watched him stand up. For the first time, she was not embarrassed to look at him closely; she even noticed curls of dark hair pushing out from under the elastic edges of his trunks. "I'm staying out here a while," she said abruptly.

"It's late, the sun's going down, you'll need to dry your hair before dinner."

"I'll be in after a while."

He stood poised over her and then, at the same moment, she closed her eyes and he dove into the water. The waves he made knocked the raft one or twice, and Vivian heard her brothers calling. She lay very still until the ripples had died down. Then she sat up to look.

The stranger boys were six feet from the raft and swimming slowly toward her. She sat looking at them cautiously, feeling a little chill as the last light slid out of the valley. When they were almost to the raft, she shivered and lay down, closing her eyes again tightly.

The raft lurched and she heard the thud of bare feet. There was a moment's silence and then someone drawled, above her, "Come on up. Nice view from here." The two in the water giggled.

"Asleep or dead?" he asked, and stubbed her arm with his toe. Vivian sat up quickly.

"I was just going in," she said.

He was a tall stark boy, rake-ribbed, his blond hair plastered to his skull with water. "How come I haven't seen you out here before?" he asked. "You staying at the lodge?"

She stood up, so close to him that her knees brushed his. Startled, she pulled back. "I'm staying here with my family," she said hotly, as though he had challenged her. Now that she was level with his face, she saw that his eyes were blue, but very pale, a strange color she had never seen before.

"Visiting from the big city?" the boy said and at the same time he shot his arm around her waist. His hand came up under her other arm and his fingers grasped her breast and molded it.

She stared into his pale blue eyes, stared and stared, as though waiting to hear him deny what he was doing. Then she began to wrench herself away. She felt each blond hair on his arm as she took her back away. Finally she darted to the edge of the raft and dove in. Coming up with a mouthful of water, she began, choking and spluttering, to swim to shore. She expected to hear them swimming after her; erratic, kicking wildly, she drove in. When she felt mud under her feet, she looked back. They were sitting on the raft, cross-legged, chattering like monkeys.

She ran up the false sand beach and snatched her towel, which lay abandoned beside her family's hollows. She wrapped the towel tightly around her shoulders as she ran, and at the same time, she began to sob. She touched the place where the boy had touched her and felt the cold wet elastic. Her breasts ached as though it had been bruised. Steve had touched her everywhere, but he had never left a trace; afterward, going over her body, she could never find a mark of what he had done. She wanted to get back to that: to wash and dry her hair and dress in her summer cotton and sit down to dinner with her parents who would not know what had happened to her. She imagined telling her father and taking shelter in his outrage, but she was afraid he would ask why she had sat up on the raft. She was afraid he would say she had invited the attack. She stopped sobbing at that. The day might come when she would want it—the muddy water and the boy on the raft and the bruised tingling in her breast. She shivered and clutched her arms, staring up at the stone bridge which still hung in sunlight. It seemed to her that she would never be safe again.

THE FROG PRINCE

Susan and her brother had been born eleven months apart and, by a coincidence which their mother considered miraculous, under the same mild and tolerating sign. When they were small, strangers often could not tell them apart, for they were both blond and slight and silent, and the differences which might have been emphasized by clothes or behavior were masked by their country uniform and their hardworking country ways. Their father believed in hardening children, especially children who would one day inherit a quantity of money, and so from an early age they raised chickens and sold eggs and planted radishes and onions as though their lives depended upon it. In the beginning, they had shared a large bedroom at the back of the house, and for a short while, they had even shared clothes, fitting into the same cotton underpants and shirts and blue jeans. Later, their mother decided that they ought to be separated, and she arranged a room for Susan with organdy curtains and a pink bedspread. After that, their similarity began slowly to dissolve. By the time she was eighteen, Susan was already tall, round, and determined, while David remained a thin stick of a boy, gentle and easily managed. They went on doing many things together, out of disheartened habit, or because nothing had replaced the old magic of association.

They had been given horses when they were small, more for the virtue inherent in cleaning out stalls than for the pleasure of riding, and they often went out together in the afternoon, threading fields and new roads and intricate subdivisions.

During the last summer before she left for college, Susan went out with David almost every day—but she cut the rides down to an hour and spent the time in silence, thinking, turning her head stubbornly away from her brother, who filled the space between them with unasked questions. He made her promise that on the last day before she left, she would take a real ride with him, a long hard ride which would cover all their old territory. Susan agreed, although she was irritated at the prospect, for David, inevitably, would take it all much too seriously. He had a way of looking at her, hungrily and confidently, as though she must know what he was feeling; yet she never knew any more, or even cared, for she was finally growing at last in her own way.

On the final day, she was late starting out to meet him at the barn. He had been there since lunch, and Susan knew he had spent all that time working on the tack, the hopeless slime-encrusted bits and the saddles white with salt. In the old days, she would have gone over early to help him, and she felt a little guilty as she came up the hill and saw him kneeling among the buckets and sponges.

"You took enough time," he said, wringing out a sponge.

"I had a lot to do." She refrained from telling him that she had spent the last half hour on the telephone; that would have made him frown. David supervised her with edgy distaste. He was usually awake when she came home at night, and she would dart across the blade of light from his door, hoping to avoid his sour, "Well, it's about time!" He had absorbed their mother's anxiety, and while she was unwilling to stay up half the night to express it, unwilling, perhaps, to make herself ridiculous with complaints, David was shameless enough to launch all her gibes. "Rolling around in the back seat again! When are you going to start to *think?*" Even when he was joking, his face did not lose its austerity; soft, ash-colored hair smudged his forehead, and inside his neat collar his neck was as thin as a bone. He seemed to have no needs, and Susan found it hard to believe that he was already seventeen. In July, he had been cornered into a blind date with a student nurse and also cornered, it seemed, into removing her clothes. He could be counted on to respond with a dazzled smile when the story was told at family lunches: how their mother had come rushing in, winged like the angel of the annunciation by her flying negligee, how the girl had cringed and whined. "But she only wanted to iron her dress," David would protest, coming in every time on cue.

He went to open the stall door and led out Susan's horse, a slab-shanked mare, slow and mean, with hazy ill-natured eyes. He held the horse while Susan mounted, and then came to shorten her stirrups. The buckle dug into the soap-softened leather, and as he pulled at it, Susan noticed how small his hands still were. "I'll do it," she said, reaching down, and then as he winced away, she sighed and waited for him to do the job himself. He adjusted the stirrup at last and passed nonchalantly in back of the mare, skirting the thick black hoofs which had caught him more than once, this time jumping out of the way with a gasp Susan almost didn't catch as the mare snorted and kicked. "When are you going to start going around the front," she said; it was no longer a question. David had played games with the mare since their father had first led her up from the trailer; it had been a sharp spring day and the mare had twirled like a top on the end of the lead rope. At the barn, their father had handed the lead to David, standing back to watch as the mare jerked up her head and the boy dropped the lead and bolted. The next day, he had bought David a horse of his own, a cinnamon-colored gelding, a biter, not a kicker.

David went to get his own horse. He was wearing jodhpur breeches and a smart tweed jacket, in spite of the heat. His clothes gave him a spurious assurance, and no one knew how often he still fell. "David is the one who has natural ability," their mother often said, watching him start out in his shining boots. Yet he seemed to have no way of gripping, and he sat the horse's high spine as though he was riding a rail.

As David slipped the bridle on, the gelding peeled back its lips and snapped. David bumped the big nose away. He did not like the horse, and once—they never referred to it—Susan had watched him take a branch and thrash the gelding's face, the horse rearing back and snorting while water streamed from its eyes. David tightened the girth and then hopped up into the saddle, his queer frog legs jutting out. With one dig, he was off at a gallop.

They went through the torn gap in the wire fence and plunged down the hill, the horses skidding and throwing up hoof-shaped clots of earth. "Wait!" Susan shouted, but David was already at the bottom of the hill, his horse sliding on the hard-surfaced road. This was not the way Susan liked to ride, jarred, losing a stirrup; she had been railing at David about it all summer. "Wait till we get to the fields!" she shouted, but David laid his heels to the gelding. The horse gathered itself up and lurched over the stream which bounded their neighbor's lawn. A little statue of a nymph, set in a bed of water lilies, fell over with a splash.

On the other side of the lawn, David pulled up. His horse had left deep marks in the fresh green sod. "Nice run," he said, patting the gelding's neck.

"Nice run!" Susan was furious. She wanted to remind him that the road was slippery and that one day he was going to fall, but his smiling assurance quelled her and she said instead, "When Mr. Baker comes out and finds these marks in his grass—"

"He's already done that a couple of times."

They rode in silence through a thicket of sycamores. It had been a dry summer and the leaves were already yellowing; the underbrush, stirred by the horses, smelled stiff and dry.

"Why do you need to go all that way to college?" David asked suddenly.

Susan had not thought of many reasons. "I don't want to live here any more, that's why," she said emphatically.

"I'd like to know what's wrong with it."

They had stopped on the brink of a shallow valley where four or five houses, brick, massive as castles, guarded their woods and lawns. "It is beautiful," Susan said, "but I don't care so much about that any more. I want to be left alone.

Mother and Daddy are always after me." She was ashamed as soon as she had said it.

"They only want you to be happy."

"They want me to wear the clothes they choose and not notice too much else."

"Nothing wrong with that. You're a pretty girl," David said dully, "you ought to want to look well. Anyway, I'm sure of one thing: you won't find people like them where you're going."

"No, I won't," she said, and thought of her mother arranging lilacs in a tall glass vase. "They're too perfect. Have you ever seen them not dressed and ready? They must go to the bathroom and brush their teeth, but somehow it doesn't show."

"I call that style," David said and cantered off. His back was very straight and Susan knew that she had offended him, rooted as he was in their parents' perfection. She pulled up beside him on the other side of the trees. "Don't they ever get at you?" she asked.

"You don't understand. They're trying to—save you from things," David said.

"Oh, don't be such a bore!" Sometimes she heard her father's voice booming inside his like an echo in a cave.

"They give me everything," he explained. "I don't have any excuse to complain. The Renault for not smoking, the lab in the basement before I even knew I was going to take that course. I never would have gotten an A last term if I hadn't had my own place to practice the experiments."

"How do other people manage, I wonder."

"I don't know. All I know is we're very lucky."

His face looked shrunken. "Is that why you let them tease you about that girl?" Susan asked.

"Who? That nurse? You don't think I was going to marry her!"

Offended again, he trotted off. As he went, his horse raised his tail and dropped two steaming turds. Susan giggled. Her brother's head was set forward like the head on a hammer.

Beyond the trees, a new road had been laid across the curve

of the hill and they heard the clank and groan of a bulldozer, rooting in a cellar hole. "I remember when there were fields all the way from here to the highway," Susan said.

"It's the Meyers's fault," David said grimly.

"Well, they couldn't live here any more, after the way they were treated."

"They could have had the decency to tell us they were selling. Daddy would have bought the land."

They plodded along in the turned earth beside the new road. "What are you going to do when it all goes?" Susan asked. "You can't be landed gentry without land."

"Our piece won't go."

"Our piece is going to look pretty small, hemmed in with subdivisions."

"You sound like you're looking forward to it."

"I remember when the first subdivision came, I wanted to kiss the ground all the way from it to our house, to hold the open fields."

"You've changed since then."

"I have other things to worry about." She did not tell him what they were.

Beyond the road, they came out into the only open land they had left: a large field, edged on all sides with trees so that it was possible to believe that beyond it lay other fields rather than houses and the highway. A milky half-moon was rising and the long grass swayed and parted as they cantered in.

David always raced in that field, letting the gelding out and leaning down like a jockey, but Susan held her mare in and jogged along slowly. When they drew up on the other side, David darted a look at her; he had won and he was flushed and smiling. The horses bent their heads to crop the weeds and still David smiled, passing his hand back and forth across his face as though to feel his satisfaction.

"If you stayed here, we could do this all the time," he said. "We could ride the way we used to, early in the morning or after supper, and you would still have plenty of time to do

crumpled lemon and a rim of
ayed at home for dinner, David
ble, and Susan watched him put
at the candle reflections in the
e that as children, passing the
David is acting a little odd?"
she thought that Susan might
efusing to go riding. Susan bit
eave a note on David's bed.
the whole morning free." But
ntil noon, and then she was

e had offered him the whole

rily. "It's too cold for you

her present: a roughrider's
reen cockade. With it, she
d would heal their breach.
r. It takes time to settle
l put it into the pocket of
ed anger, as he used to be
ey instead of a present.
ng that she had made a
ox and took out the hat.
en, but later in the day
e hall mirror with the

l the countryside froze,
er. The magnolias had
nd now the snow bent
und. All day, Susan's
ing off the accumula-

ol, and he drank his
sing through, Susan
to take me riding?"

other things. We could find a new way under the highway and
explore those fields on the other side. . . ."

"And you could win all the races."

"If you kept your horse exercised regularly, it wouldn't be
any time before you offered me some serious competition."

She wanted to ask him if he really thought she could make
a life out of that, but again his strange smiling certainty
silenced her, as though he might really be the one who knew.
So she only said, "It's too late now to change my mind," and as
soon as she had said it, she realized how fragile his certainty
was; he stopped smiling and jerked at the reins.

They had reached the limit of their ride; now, they were on
their way home. As they picked along a paved road, the sound
of the horses' hoofs roused children and dogs. Archaic, a little
ridiculous, they rode by stiff-backed. "Hey, mister, can I pat
the horse?" a boy impudently cried, running almost between
the gelding's legs.

"Get back if you don't want to get hurt," David snapped, and
Susan was united with him in disdain of this new-come life, the
barbecue pits, the false brick façades, and the cheeky children
who would never know anything about horses.

It was dark when they came back to the barn, and they un-
saddled and rubbed down the horses without bothering to
light a lantern. Susan finished first; she was in a hurry to bring
the afternoon to an end. In an hour, she would have to be ready
to go out to dinner. It was not only a question of washing and
changing her clothes, but of stripping off her brother's ways.
"Are you finished?" she called to him.

"No. That's all right, you go on back."

She listened for a minute to the scrape of his brush. Then,
as she left the barn, she felt, for the first time, free to go, free,
almost, to forget him.

There was a small square of greasy grass in front of the dor-
mitory where Susan spent the autumn. On her first evening
there, she looked out at the grass and thought that it could

represent for her all the open spaces she had left behind. Wh
she sat looking out the window, the light slowly failed,
when it was dark, she went to bed, for there were no light b
in her lamps.

Later, she forgot about the little yard, which turned to
under the first rains. The house where she had gro
seemed far away and she was not eager to make comp
She spent a great deal of time watching people, spendi
evening in the library, where boys and girls sat toget
legs entwined under the tables. She noticed that, sur
yet relieved. She did not try to speak to anyone, f
begun to feel that there was something so different
so conspicuously lacking or so excessive—she didn't
—that they couldn't have liked her, if they had
though she was not unhappy, she found herself
verge of tears and she hated that; what was the u
made her eyes stick out like a frog's. Yet even the
hands of a boy and a girl in the library reduced

She went home for Christmas gratefully as
going back into the honeycomb. She looke
luxury of that remote and comfortable hous
smile wordlessly at her parents and be und
where she could lie in bed all morning an
over her, softly, like bare feet. She did no
she had left him where she expected to fi
beginning, he was angry with her.

He came to the airport with their pa
as soon as he saw her, he frowned. "I kr
her off with one hand. "Knee socks an

Her father laughed. "We'll strip h
home."

The three of them chattered all
David sat in silence. Susan found h
she had spent away, for his benefit.
enough, and so she added color: w
at which she had reaped a whirl
at involvements, intrigues, shook her ne

upon the remains of his te
unbuttered toast. When she
sat in his old place across the
his eyes out of focus, staring
mahogony. They had both do
dreary time. "Don't you think
she asked her mother, who said
have been more tactful about r
off her surprise and went to
"What about tomorrow? I have
David told her he had classes u
tied up for lunch.
"I'm sorry," she said, wishing sl
day.
"That's all right," he said ang
anyway."
On Christmas day, she gave him
hat, the brim pinned up with a g
handed him a note which she hope
"Have a little mercy on your sist
down." David read the note first and
his robe. He was faceless with repress
when his godmother sent him mon
"Open the box," Susan urged, realizi
mistake. At last he broke open the b
He did not express much enthusiasm t
Susan saw him standing in front of t
hat perched jauntily on his head.
It snowed the following morning an
cracked and singed by the excessive win
already been scorched by an early frost a
the box bushes, splitting them to the gr
mother went around with a broom, knoc
tion.
David was late coming home from sch
tea standing up at the kitchen table. Pa
asked reproachfully, "When are you going

and then went on without waiting for an answer, a little ashamed of her coyness. He had turned to answer her, his face brightening and then dwindling again into its usual pallor. There was something about him which made Susan angry, as though he needed, in their mother's words, a good hiding to cheer him up. Later, when she saw him leaving for the barn, she threw open the window, tempted to call out to him to wait. David stopped and turned, and as he looked up at her, Susan remembered a picture she had seen long ago of a frog prince staring up at a lady in a tower. "Have a good time," she called for lack of anything better, and then she bowed back in, shivering and rubbing her arms.

It was dark by five o'clock. From her window, Susan saw the elm trees bar the red horizon. The house was still except for the clucking of the radiators, and as Susan began to lay out her clothes for the evening, she wondered if she would ever be able to go away again. The telephone rang distantly in her mother's room and after a moment, she heard a scurrying sound in the hall. Her mother waded in, knocking over a chair. "Mrs. Baker says we have to go down to the road."

"But I'm not dressed."

"We have to go down to the road," her mother repeated, and went out. After a minute, Susan huddled her coat around her shoulders and followed. She did not understand why her mother looked wildly harassed, as she had all day, knocking the snow out of the box bushes. They got into the car and drove down the hill. At the bottom, Susan saw David's gelding, standing beside a tree. There was a slick of ice across the road and on it she saw her brother's hat.

He had fallen on the road and he still lay on his back, one arm up as though he was saluting.

THE NEED

After two years at home, Alice King decided that she had had enough. She had been living with her father, in her own little apartment, actually, at the top of the house, ever since she graduated from college. Her father was a widower, and his delight at Alice's return had seemed to outweigh the pleasure she might have taken in graduate school, or even in a year abroad. It was not, after all, a bad arrangement; she saw to his meals and clothes, as she had always done, worked five days a week at the bookstore in town, and made efforts to know a variety of people. Several young men had asked her to marry them, or at least to agree to an affair, and she had agreed, more or less, in one case. But before long, the affair had begun to be a harassment; she had no privacy, and she couldn't even find time to wash her hair. Then spring came on and she began to gain weight and to feel restless. So she finally decided. She was only twenty-three, yet her life was a little laborious: everything was done for a reason, to fill a gap. She decided to let the gap loom a little, or at least to fill it with something else.

When she asked her father if she could go, he turned away brusquely and said he had never expected her to stay so long. She put her arms around him and admitted that she was asking a great deal, of herself as well as of him. She was ready to give it all up, if he said the word. But after a while he began to urge her to take her life into her own hands, and she realized with a start that he would not entirely miss her. While she had been away at college, he had grown quite slovenly, and he would relish lying in bed again and changing his underwear only every other day.

So she did not expect to feel much of a wrench when she finally left. Yet as she turned around to wave, on the airplane steps, she almost groaned. Her father was standing beside the gate, waiting patiently for her to disappear so that he could climb into his car and go home. She realized that she would never be able to go back to him and so she groaned, not because of her obligation to him but because of the space opening up around it.

In New York, she found a job in a bookstore, poorly paid but promising, and she rented a little apartment with the kitchen in a closet, considerably less attractive than her apartment in her father's house. Then she set about making herself some kind of life. But it was hard to meet people in the city— everything had to be planned—and then, it was really the first time she had lived alone. She could not help feeling that she was entirely vulnerable, peeled, like an egg, and when taxi drivers were rude to her, as they often were, she took their remarks meekly, as her due.

It was not long before she began to be lonely, and she recognized the danger in that. She was always noticing men, on the subway or in shops, and she was afraid of developing a ferocious gleam. Sometimes she hummed over her cart in the supermarket and picked out with aplomb the doll-sized jars of jam and the dwarf breadloaf which fitted her solitary life; but then she would notice someone on the street, too vividly, and realize that the gap was still there, waiting to be filled. So she set about finding a man. She had no distinct physical craving. But she wanted to be able to spoil herself, to eat well and sleep long, justifiably. She wanted the pleasure of herself, the pride and the luxury, which she had felt once or twice when she was in bed with a man.

She had several irons in the fire when she met Tom O'Connor, and she knew at once that he would not do. He was too short, for one thing—"*Never* tower," her father had warned her—too blond and frail, like a sickly, handsome child. And

then, he had no manners; he hardly noticed her. They met at
a party where no one seemed to know anyone else, and Alice
thought that Tom, too, was ill at ease. But when she asked
him, "Who are all these people, anyway?" he scowled at her.
He did not want to be classed with a girl from Illinois, he,
with his careful little feet and his broad flowered tie. "You're a
pretty girl but you really ought to grow your hair," he said
spitefully.

"Don't you want to see the back of my neck?" She turned her
head obligingly.

"You're not from here, are you?"

"No, but I will be someday."

"What about having dinner," he said vaguely.

"No, thanks; you're not my type." She was really a little
frightened. He seemed aimed, in spite of his vagueness.

"Are you doing something else?"

Her lies deserted her and she felt pressed, alarmed. Yet in
spite of herself, she was pleased, and she couldn't stop smiling
at him. Satisfied, he went off to talk to someone else, and she
had to remind him of his promise when it was time to leave.

He shuffled her into her coat and took her elbow as though
she were an invalid, precious, but a bore. In the taxi, he gave
the name of a restaurant without asking her first where she
wanted to go. She never knew where she wanted to go, yet she
expected to be asked, and she began to feel rushed again,
breathless and pleased. Although it was a cheap little place
with plastic flowers against the walls, Tom spent a great deal
of time on the menu and sent the Chianti back. He hardly
spent any time on Alice, having ordered for her and seen that
she was served. After a long silence, she excused herself and
went into the ladies' room to see if she looked as bad as he was
treating her. I must make more effort, she thought, and she
spread lipstick across her mouth in a pale broad band. Then
she came back and began to try to amuse him. After all, she
had a small town and a doting father to draw on for material.
Tom did not pay much attention; now and then he glanced at
her, smiled, and nodded affably. He seemed to have disappeared

into his preoccupations, and only his ears, his sharp-tipped, tiny ears, were available.

"You don't have to try so hard. I'm already won," he said suddenly, and she gasped at his clairvoyance and subsided into embarrassed silence. At last he began to play with her, flattering her with insults and doling out information. "I like you!" she cried at one point, remembering that she, too, could charm.

"I like you too, but you ought to grow your hair."

"Well, I'm going to grow it." She couldn't help asking, "Am I so ugly, this way?"

He looked at her, openly speculating, and then he beckoned to the waiter for the bill. Alice was still waiting for his reply as she followed him out of the restaurant. In the taxi, she heard him give an address with a sense of fatality.

"We're going to my place," he explained.

"What do you expect me to do there?"

He burst out laughing and kissed her neck.

His apartment was not at all what she had expected. He had money—that was one of the facts he had divulged—yet he lived in ordinary squalor, like a college boy. The desk was coated with dust and cigarette ashes and there were clothes all over the dirty Mexican rug. Tom did not even offer her a drink or five minutes' talk to pad the occasion. She had an uneasy feeling that the sheets on his bed were not clean, and the effort to dominate this unworthy scruple left her limp in his hands. He undressed her, looked at her, and sent her off to the bathroom. When she came back, clutching a towel, he was lying on the bed, reading. He put a match in the book and made room for her.

He hardly touched her, he passed over her so quickly. He did not seem to notice her, in detail; her hips and breasts were obstacles, to be surmounted. "Pretty," he said, but his hands flashed over her quickly, and he spoke out of obligation, huskily. She began to feel that she was a mountain over which he was obliged to labor. In the end, he disengaged himself quickly and sent her off to the bathroom with an affectionate little tap. When she came back, after standing for several

minutes, distracted, by the sink—for what after all did he expect her to do?—he asked, "Will you spend the night?" His
voice was casual and yet she thought she heard the concern she
had missed in his touch, and she lay down and pressed her face
into his shoulder. "I'll stay as long as you like," she said, and
she began to relax a little, she lay into him, sighing.

In the morning, she woke with a jerk, frightened to find herself in a strange room. Then she began to look around. The
closet door was open and inside she could see the clothes he
wore to other meetings, for other purposes. His shoes were
scrambled on the floor and there were ties on all the chairs.
The disorder bothered Alice; it seemed so permanent. He
would always leave her to return to this private chaos. Suddenly she saw herself compelled to scurry around, picking
things up and emptying ash trays. At that, she got out of bed
and began to put on her rumpled clothes. Going into the bathroom, she stared at her face in the mirror as though the arrangement of her features had betrayed her, as though the space
between her pale blue eyes had invited the poleax. Then she
heard Tom get out of bed. "Good morning," she called cheer-
fully, knowing what was expected of her.

He came quickly into the bathroom. "I thought you had
gone," he said. "Why did you just get up like that?" Alice
laughed and put her arms around him. His back was rake-
ribbed, fragile, and he seemed suddenly very small. She knew
as she held him that it was not sex which had led her to him
but the siren song of his need, the faint reminiscent roar, like
the sea-roar in a shell, of his weakness and lack. It was a great
relief to her to know that. She held him for a while and then
he dressed and they went out to have breakfast, holding hands
for the first time.

All day, at work, she prevented herself from calling him, although her life had unraveled and the loose ends floated, waiting to be caught up. That evening, she expected him to call,
she even thought of a place where they could have dinner, but
when he did not, she cooked herself an omelet, read ten pages
of a novel, and finally washed her hair. As she was drying it,

she began to sob, and she leaned against the towel rack and let herself go. After a while, she went to the telephone and dialed his number. It rang and rang. She thought of his suits in the closet; his life seemed rich and varied and she knew her place in it. At last she bribed herself to sleep with the promise that when he went to bed and saw her blond hairs on the pillow, he would be bound to remember.

Waking the next morning, she heard the pigeons cooing in the warm spring sun; the best half of the year was beginning, and she resolved with some finality to be equal to it. She would not telephone him, she would not humble herself; after all, she had her whole life, her whole dutiful honest twenty-three years to live up to, and there were many reasons to be proud. First of all, there was her skin, and her hair. She had always been known for her fine skin and her short blond hair. They were distinctions; her whole past life was an obligation to elevate the present. In college, she had read every book which had been assigned to her, she had even worked her way through the collateral and supplementary lists, yet somehow she had avoided the reputation of brilliance: she had never really seemed to try. At home she had worked diligently at the bookstore, and she had never allowed herself to become too dependent on her father, although everyone told her how good he was, how gentle and kind. Now in New York she had a respectable job, and she was trying to make herself a life. And there were also other reasons to be proud. First of all, there was her skin, and her hair. Her father had always admired her hair. Once long ago, she had asked him in a kind of agony if she was pretty, and he had answered, after some deliberation, "You have very nice hair." Her father had always supported and praised her, yet he had been careful too about setting limits. Years ago, when he had been particularly sweet to her, Alice had tried to climb up on his lap. She winced, remembering that; what a great gawky thing she must have been! She could still feel the way his knees had stiffened. "Alice . . . get down, Alice." He had spoken patiently, with distaste, as he spoke to the dogs when they jumped up. They could be excused, but she should have understood. The limits he had set were always clear and reasonable. Then why had she failed to understand? It frightened her to remember how she had surged against him. Was there some frenzy in her, some bestiality?

In the evening, she went to the movies, and when she came back, she covered the telephone with a flowered towel.

Three days later, Tom was waiting for her when she came out of the bookstore. She caught sight of him over the crowd and, waving and smiling, she began to make her way toward him. He pushed energetically too, cutting his way across the current of people. When they reached each other, there was nothing to say. They gripped hands and smiled, dazzled by the fatality of the meeting. Afterward, in his bed, Alice felt for the first time that he was touching her, and the relief and delight of it reminded her of the first time she had gone dancing and felt a boy's arms around her and known that it was all right.

After that, they set up a routine which allowed them both a certain amount of privacy and rest. They had dinner together on Tuesdays and Thursdays, and they spent most of their weekends in Tom's apartment, eating odd meals at odd times, wearing fragments of clothes. Of course it was not quite enough. Alice searched the newspapers for concerts, movies, plays, and even the minor holidays provided her with excuses. They both joked about these infractions of their discipline. They liked to be busy together, to appear to have plans, and their routines were nearly always energetic and gay. Yet at the end of the evening, a silence would settle over them, a thickening sense of threat. For then it had to be decided whether or not they would make love. It was almost a relief to Alice when Tom said, "God, I'm tired, I really need some sleep." Then she could reply, "I'm just dead, too," and they would talk about other things all the way to her building. It seemed to extend their relationship, to forgo sex. After all, they shared so many other things.

They never quarreled. Only once, when Tom went away for the weekend to visit his mother, Alice grew impatient. His mother lived outside of Boston in a big comfortable house—

Tom had shown her a snapshot—and Alice imagined waking up there in a four-poster bed, having her breakfast on a tray, and finally emerging to admiring eyes. Of course, she did not say anything about it, but she was a little snappish with Tom on the day he left. He stared at her when she snapped at him about something. That Saturday, Alice realized that there was no longer anything she wanted to do alone. That frightened her—she had never let herself go so far before—and when Tom came back on Monday, she made an angry scene. Afterward, she tried to be calm and ask reasonable questions, but his answers seemed hideously abstract. Yes, his mother was well and the weather had been beautiful. It was all of a piece with what he had told her before, with the curious vacuity of his life. His mother was a widow who lived outside of Boston and his sister was a schoolteacher who lived in Cincinnati. Even his adolescence, from his account, had been placid and uneventful. From the beginning, Alice had admired his coolness, and yet now she felt that she was being cheated, that he was keeping her away from everything that mattered, keeping her hands off his life.

He made love to her to compensate for the two days he had been away; whenever Alice looked at him, his eyes were closed. She could not remember whether he usually closed his eyes, and because she could not be sure and could not ask, she felt as though she herself had gone blind. He continued to operate on her, but she could not feel him; he had no substance, no taste or smell, he was as empty as air. Like the misted, colorless city sky, the embalmed trees in the park, and the glare of the obscured sun, he passed into an abstraction, he became a sign for something else. Tom finished and went to the bathroom, and Alice got out of bed.

The room was in its usual disorder. She had been less bothered by it recently, but now she kicked his books and shoes out of the way in a fury. Then she went to his desk and began to open the drawers. There was nothing in them but snapshots, bland letters and bank statements. In the end, she took the drawers out one by one and emptied them onto the floor. Then she dropped to her knees and began to rake through the pile of paper. But there was nothing to be found except snapshots, telegrams, litter. When Tom came out of the bathroom, she began to rail at him—something about his untidiness. She did not understand how he could bear to keep everything, and then it was all so ordinary, so trivial and boring! While she railed, he stood in the doorway and watched her attentively, as though she might spring. "I know it's not enough, but there's nothing more I can do," he said, dully and smoothly, when she stopped to breathe.

"Well then, I'm wasting my time here." She scrabbled up and lunged for her coat, and he came quietly and helped her into it. "I'm sorry," he said, and she noticed how tired he looked, wax-colored, as though he had lost blood. She did not dare to wait until her anger ran down, and she bolted down three flights of stairs without waiting to hear the door close behind her.

She had to be free of him, she knew that; she had to break loose. He would blind her with his vagueness, crush her under the weight of his strange unconcern. Yet when she looked at the only snapshot she had of him, his pale face, in the midst of dead park greenery, seemed too small a target for her rage. She had no life, no wishes, apart from him. It rained that evening, and as she stood at her window and looked out over the streaming city, Alice thought that she might have been saved. The cool rain seemed to bless her hands as she stretched them out on the gritty sill. The city began to stir again after the silence of the storm, and she listened to the gay bleat of taxis in the street and tried to believe that her whole life still lay in front of her, tried to remember how lively she had felt, how hungry, even, when the city first spread before her eyes.

In the flush of success, she telephoned Tom and told him that she had decided not to see him for a while. She had been treasuring the threat for some time, and now she offered it to him proudly, expecting an outburst. He sighed, and told her that she was doing the right thing. "I knew from the start I couldn't give you whatever it is you want," he said. She was angry at him for being so reasonable, and she said with ironic caution, "It's only life I want." She hung up, and then as his voice began to fall away into the past, the unreachable past where her life seemed to lie buried, she began to sink into silence and despair. Night came on, and she stood by the window, watching lights prick on in the park. There were voices, and the slight dusty smell of city leaves, and car lights passing quickly up the street, but it did not occur to her that she could go out and walk among the people on the sidewalk. After a while, it was as though her bones had melted together. She was rigid, placed, as though she would never move again, and it occurred to her that she herself was the eye of the target, fixed and vulnerable to the flight of her own arrows. Suddenly she remembered the long evenings of her childhood, when she had sat by her window, waiting for the lights from her father's car.

Thinking of that, she began to move slowly across the room, placing one foot in front of the other cautiously. Her joints seemed welded together and her hands hung at the ends of her arms like stones. So she moved, slowly and carefully, toward the telephone.

He answered at once, as though he had been waiting, and Alice was pleased to imagine that he had waited for a long time. When she looked at her watch, she saw that in fact it had only been three hours since she had stormed out of his room, and she wondered if it was enough to be proud of, enough to remember: that she had resisted, at least, for three hours. He said that he would come over at once, and while she waited for him, she went over her arguments, curiously, as though someone else had made them. When she opened the door, he stepped inside and stood with his hands in his raincoat pockets. "It still won't be enough," he said.

She huddled him into her arms. He drew his head back to look at her. "You must understand something, if we're going to begin again. We can't have any more scenes."

Tears ran down her cheeks as she hastened to reassure him. "I know I'm too demanding, I know I want too much."

He took hold of her suddenly and squeezed her arms. "Don't stop," he said. "Don't stop." And then it was her turn to comfort him.

The rest of the summer passed busily enough. Tom even took her to the seashore for a weekend. Then cold weather came, with its larger opportunities, and gradually the summer evening was buried under a silt of details, shared experiences neither of them cared to examine. Tom came down with a serious cold at the beginning of the autumn, and after that, he often seemed tired. Alice fell into the habit of taking his laundry for him and doing his shopping; she picked out bunches of grapes and fresh green chives. One Saturday, she decided to tidy his room. As she was piling up the books, she began to sing, and Tom watched her from the couch with his mild, vague eyes. She smiled at him, and then laughed, seeing them as they would be in a photograph: he on the couch, his long pale hair curling over his ears, and she in her gingham apron, singing and gathering up the fragments of his life.

MOURNING

Waiting for the plane that was bringing home her parents and her sister's body, Ellen Cage had a chance to look around the airport. It had changed in the ten years since she had been returning to it regularly, from school and college. There were large glass windows set into the walls, containing displays of local products—lumber, steel, and whisky—and the folding chairs she remembered, scattered chaotically, had been replaced by long soft couches, upholstered in tweed. In the mild draft from the air-conditioning system, long-leafed plants stirred and bowed. There had been so many changes that Ellen looked out of the window several times, simply to reassure herself. There, the sallow wheat fields, recently harvested, spread in grainy patterns over the low hills, and even the rearing trunk of a red threshing machine did nothing more than contrast with the plain yellow poverty of the place. Ellen had left in order to live, or at least to live better, and it was a relief to find that only the airport had improved.

After half an hour of walking and looking, she felt someone touch her arm and recognized the broad damp face of the minister who had officiated at all the family weddings and baptisms. "Ellen, so terrible," he said. She had the strange notion that he was going to take her in his arms, and involuntarily she stepped back. "Can I get you something, a Coke or something?" he asked.

She realized that she must look as hot as he did and took a handkerchief from her purse to wipe her face. "No, thank you.

This air conditioning had me fooled; I thought it was cold in here." She laughed and looked at him again. Even at the marriages, he had had a hangdog look, as though such festivities invited disaster, and when he had christened her nieces and nephews, Ellen had seen the bundles of lace quivering in his arms. Feeling sorry for him, she asked how he was, and saw that once again she had said the wrong thing.

"I was wondering about you," he said humbly. "The terrible shock. And then the trip down here alone."

"It's only an hour by jet."

"The terrible shock," he repeated sadly.

"She never was a good swimmer. I remember when we were little, she was always fussing around at the deep ends of pools, falling in, screaming, being yanked out. When she took lessons, she cried and wouldn't go near the water but when she was on her own, she fell in all the time."

"Those beaches should be closed. They say the undertow is fierce. And there've been . . ." He hesitated. "Shark warnings."

"You mean she's not coming home in one piece?"

"No, no." He patted her arm. "I gather they found her in quite shallow water."

"She could drown in anything, a teacup."

"Shock does such strange things to people," he remarked, prying his tight collar away from his neck. "It's something I always notice. They start to talk about the most irrelevant things. I often feel it's my job to bring them back on target."

She disliked him then and was glad he had never been called upon to marry her, although that had been, for years, one of her dreams. She had liked to think of his sad face bent over her, warning, admonishing, in the midst of the crackle of silk and the smell of hyacinths.

"I hope I haven't offended you," he said.

"When is the plane coming?"

He went to ask someone behind a desk and returned quickly to tell her that the tower was already in contact.

The walked to the plate-glass window that faced the airfield. Reaching out, Ellen touched the glass; it was warm and dusty. With one finger, she traced a design in front of her face, a large open tulip. She focused her eyes through the extended petals and saw the airstrip clearly. At the far end, a small plane was setting down. It taxied toward them, tame as a dog.

"Shall we go out?" Reverend Black was holding open the door.

The heat from the concrete rushed up into Ellen's face and she held her breath, adjusting. Then she followed the minister to the steps of the plane. The propellers were still turning idly, and she thought that, at least for a while, no one would be allowed to get off. Then the passenger door was thrust open, and her mother stepped out. She held a book in one hand and her purse in the other, and she came down the steps one by one as though balancing on a rope. At the bottom, she held out her arms, and Ellen embraced her and kissed her soft dry cheek.

Her father came down next; he was carrying a suitcase. "Ellen," he said, and he put down the suitcase and took her tightly in his arms. She had to remind herself not to pull back, and, for confidence, she tried to remember when he had held her like that before; perhaps when she had left the first time for New York. Finally, he let her go, and she picked up the suitcase.

"I've got the car out front," she said. "They let me park in the taxi place since there weren't any taxis."

"There never are," her father said. "At least when you want them, they're never there."

Her mother went on ahead, still balancing carefully. Reverend Black had put his hand under her arm.

Inside the terminal, the cool breeze lifted her father's hair and Ellen noticed how pink his scalp was, like a baby's. "How long did the flight take?" she asked.

"We were delayed in Boston. Fog, we couldn't get through. We sat for an hour and forty minutes and then they got us out."

"Did you have any lunch?"

"I had a chicken sandwich, but your mother wouldn't eat."

"There's some cheese in the refrigerator. Cheese and beer. I looked before I came out. Will that do?"

"Oh, Ellen," he said. "I'm so glad you're here. I had a horrible feeling you wouldn't be able to make it."

"I'm bad but not that bad. When are the boys coming?"

"They're flying in this afternoon. Peter's wife had to stay at home with the children, but everyone else will be here."

They went out of the terminal building and hesitated in the heavy glare. Then Ellen opened the door of the car and helped her mother in; she felt light and limp, like a rag doll. Reverend Black held the back door open for Mr. Cage, who seemed about to protest; felled by the heat, he bowed in.

"I'll be right behind you," the minister promised and hurried away to his car.

Ellen climbed into the driver's seat and started the motor. Next to her, her mother was arranging her purse and her book; Ellen caught sight of her white-gloved hands, scuttling along like crabs. She remembered the feeling of those hands, in her hair, on her face, patting, correcting, never still except when they lay like shells on the turned-down sheet. It had not occurred to Ellen that her mother would be the same, after what had happened, and she felt choked with rage, suddenly, as though nobody cared.

Her father was looking out of the window. "They're taking her straight to Mason's," he said. "I wanted to take her home first, but they said it wouldn't be practical. Mason's men are here to take her."

"Yes, I saw their truck," Ellen said.

"Not truck," her mother whispered.

"It looked like a truck, except it was painted black. I saw one of their men, too, lurking behind a palm."

Mr. Cage went on, "They'll bring her home tomorrow. Ten o'clock in the morning, they said."

"All neat and clean and ready for the festivities."

Ellen's mother sat up stiffly. "This is one time I am not going to stand your tongue. You can talk that way all you want to in New York. I'm not going to stand it here now."

"We thought about having the funeral tomorrow," Mr. Cage

explained quickly, "but it seemed too soon. We knew people would want a chance to come by the house, first."

"The front hall is nearly full of flowers already," Ellen said.

Mrs. Cage nodded. "And so many are from *her* friends."

"What made her go swimming at five o'clock in the morning?"

Mrs. Cage looked at her. "It was six o'clock. Mrs. Chrysler is sure she heard her go. The gate to the stairs down the dunes makes a click that wakes her. She's a very light sleeper, always has been."

"Six, then. Is it that hot on Martha's Vineyard?"

"It wasn't the heat. Susie had been up all night, working."

"Working!"

Her mother smiled. "You don't know about her newest project. She's doing a piece on primitive man, I mean his customs and so on. Mrs. Chrysler showed me the books. There must have been a dozen."

"So she got tired of primitive man and went for a dip."

"Yes, that's it," her father agreed. "She's so intense, I can see her getting tied up on a point, getting stuck because a sentence wasn't coming out right—"

"And just going down and throwing herself into the ocean."

There was a pause. "You don't understand," her mother said. "She was going swimming."

"In her bathing cap and her red bikini?"

"She was naked when they found her." Her mother began to weep; she held her fingers up to catch the tears. "It was several hours later. The sea had pulled off her clothes."

"So she went swimming in her clothes at five in the morning."

"I told you, *six!* Mrs. Chrysler heard the gate."

"And never thought to look out."

Her mother began to rub her hands. "I know what you want now. You want to blame me. You think if she'd stayed in that place—"

"It had some nice trees. I remember them."

"She couldn't be kept under lock and key all her life," Mr.

Cage said softly. "We had to take some risks. Her doctor told us that."

"He said a year, do you remember that? At least a year before she could even try to manage alone."

Mrs. Cage reached for the door handle. "I tell you I am not going to stand this. If you want to go on like this, you can let me out."

Ellen slowed down the car.

"Ellen, please." Her father's voice was thick.

She pressed her foot down on the accelerator and they drove for a while in silence. In the rear-view mirror, she caught sight of the minister's small green car, hurrying along behind them. She looked at her mother. "I guess you should have gone with Reverend Black. He always seems to know what to say."

"He has been a great help," her mother said. Her voice was calm again and she was looking straight ahead. Only her cheeks were still flushed, as though the tears had rubbed them. "He came to the house yesterday as soon as we called him."

"I had to be on the telephone all the time," Mr. Cage explained. "There were so many people to contact, your aunts, your cousins, and, of course, your brothers. There would have been no one to sit with your mother."

"What did you talk about?" Ellen asked.

"He mainly read prayers."

Ellen tried to imagine her mother down on her knees on the red-and-green rug. She remembered lying on that rug as a child, counting the green leaves while her father read aloud. The memory relieved her of her rage, and she felt for the first time as though she might be going to cry. "I don't know anything about being consoling," she said, pressing her fingers tightly around the damp steering wheel. "I thought about that on the plane. I don't know anything about how to make people feel better."

"Nobody can make me feel better," her mother said.

"Just having you here . . ." Her father's voice ran down. It had sounded strange from the beginning, when he had telephoned her: low, flat, even, with all the thrills and frills pressed out. It was not the voice of grief, as Ellen had imagined it, but a dull mechanical patter. Suddenly it occurred to her that he was always holding down sobs.

They were nearly home. Ellen turned into their street and looked at the white frame houses set in broad hedged lawns. The heat had scorched the grass and the trees, and even the houses looked singed. In the taxi that morning, driving home from the airport, she had thought that the whole street looked burned, but now she noticed the gleaming white railings and the late roses, blooming undisturbed. She turned the car into the driveway and stopped in front of the garage, feeling for the place where she had always parked. The branches of a weeping willow brushed the glass beside her face and, remembering the warning, she climbed out of the car as cautiously as though her parents were still asleep in the big bedroom upstairs.

They walked together up the brick path to the kitchen door. The honeysuckle on the porch was still blooming. "I don't remember ever seeing it bloom this late," Ellen said.

"We had a late spring," her mother replied.

They went inside. Ellen heard the refrigerator click and begin to whir. The kitchen smelled of floor polish and overripe apples. She saw the apples in a bowl on the table; her mother had neglected to put them away. Ellen went over and chose one. It was a little soft, and nearly brown. She sank her teeth into it, tasting the mealy sweetness, next to rottenness. Juice trailed down her chin.

"I didn't eat on the plane," she explained.

"Neither have I. It's been hours." Her mother pulled open the refrigerator door. Reaching in, she seized a package of cheese and tore off the top of the wrapper. Jerking up two slices, she began to eat, standing at the open refrigerator.

"Sit down," her husband pleaded, nudging at her.

"It's cool here," she said.

Reverend Black tapped softly on the screen door, and Mrs. Cage thrust the cheese back in the refrigerator. She turned toward the minister, brushing her hands on her skirt. "Come in, we have a lot to talk about. Shall we go to the living room?"

Her head high, she led the way, the two men following behind. Ellen finished her apple and threw the core away.

Her father put his head around the door. "You coming, Ellen?"

She went with him.

By four o'clock that afternoon, everyone had arrived. Ellen's older brothers, Art and Peter, came on separate planes, and Ellen spent the afternoon driving back and forth between the house and the airport. Everyone cried when they saw her; even Peter's glasses misted up, and he hawked and bowed on her shoulder. Art's wife, four months pregnant, was blown and pale with tears; Art told Ellen privately that she hadn't stopped since morning.

At the house, the telephone was ringing constantly. Someone had to sit by it all the time with a pencil and pad, to write down the names of the callers. Peter took over the job as soon as he walked in; he spoke discreetly and dryly and knew when it was time to bring the call to an end. "We all appreciate . . . ," he would begin, and then Ellen would know he was about to hang up. His list was neatly written and the names were correctly spelled. Once, Art's wife answered the telephone, but she burst into tears; that was the end of it for her and she was sent upstairs to rest.

Art was stationed at the front door to receive callers, casseroles, and flowers. Most people insisted on coming to the back —the door closest to the drive—and so Art was constantly going to and fro, his face set with heat and frustration. Ellen heard him once at the back door, begging, "Can't you go around front? We're all set up there." The card basket was there, a silver-and-enamel bowl that Ellen remembered had always held candies, as well as a row of vases which her mother had filled. By the end of the afternoon the house was swollen with flowers; all white, in massive heaps and towers, they crowded the little hall, the living room, the dining room, and finally the kitchen. Their smell, a heavy sweet reek, reached up the stairs and penetrated into the bedroom where Art's wife had begun to throw up. Art said it was morning sickness. "In the afternoon, and all afternoon," Mrs. Cage remarked.

She had changed into a crisp black linen dress, and she sat at the desk in her bedroom, writing notes. Every hour, she asked for the telephone list to be brought up and examined the names with interest. Ellen noticed that she was keeping some sort of tabulation on a pad. The flowers meant less to her— "Anybody can call up and order flowers"—but now and then she asked for the bowl of cards.

At four-thirty, Mr. Cage and the minister went out to make arrangements. Ellen did not understand what the arrangements were until her father came back.

"I had to choose the coffin, you see," he explained. He was standing in the hall, beside the flower table; tall delphinium spikes loomed over his head. "We went to Mason's, and they took us to a room where they have all the different types. Mr. Mason showed me the one I chose for my father. He said he was sure I would want to do as well by Susan. It had silver handles."

"Do they leave the handles on?"

"I don't know. I didn't think of that. The inside is sort of quilted."

"So that's the one you got?"

"Yes." He seemed about to sink. Ellen took his hand and led him into the living room.

"What happened to her, Daddy?"

He stared at her wearily. "Nobody knows. Nobody will ever know, I guess."

"But can't you find out? Can't you ask somebody how she seemed?"

"There isn't anybody to ask, except Mrs. Chrysler."

"Didn't anybody else see her, up there?"

"Well, no, I guess not. Susie's always been sort of shy. But you know, her letters were marvelous: every week, six or seven pages. She was describing the island for us, in detail. First the town itself, which she didn't care for, and then the artists' colony out at the far end. She was really very funny describing the types she saw there; pretty outlandish, I gather."

Ellen wanted to shake him. She stepped so close that her breasts brushed his tie. "I want to know what happened to her."

Peter, at the telephone, covered the mouthpiece. "I can't hear anything with all this noise."

Ellen took hold of her father and pulled him into the dining room. His arm, inside the loose sleeve, was thin and pliable. She backed him up against the sideboard to begin again, and then she saw that he was weeping.

"Please, don't start that," she said, sobbing a little. "I want to ask you something."

"Can't you leave me alone?" he pleaded thinly. "Isn't it bad enough that it's happened? Do you have to keep on prying?"

Ellen turned away and stared at her mother's silver tea set, flashing in the hot light from the bay window. "I have to find out," she said. "There's nothing else for me to do here."

"Well, not from me. Go ask your mother, if you have to find out. She's the one who talked to Mrs. Chrysler."

"Where were you?"

"Oh, leave me alone, Ellen," he rasped, turning away.

She started doggedly toward the stairs. Art, rushing to the back door, brushed against her and glared. "Can't you help me out with this?"

"In a minute." She noticed that he was carrying a large yellow casserole.

In the upstairs hall, snapshots of the four of them hung in red frames on the white wall. Ellen stopped to look for her own face, narrow and plain, hidden like a thorn among the others. She found herself in a party dress with a blue sash; Susie's sash was pink. Then there was a snapshot of her in a pony class. The last picture was the one of her graduation. After that, her face was missing from the ranks, which began to include weddings and new babies. She hurried on toward her mother's room.

On the way, she passed the door to Susie's room and hesitated, looking in. The canopied bed was curtained with veils of organdy, and the dressing table was hung with lace, like an altar. Stepping inside, she was surprised by the neatness; there was only a nail file and a bottle of perfume to prove that the room had been occupied. On the table beside the bed, she saw a copy of Susie's high-school yearbook, its blue cover worn and faded. Opening it, she turned to her sister's page and stared at the small blond face, pointed like a heart. "She walks in beauty, like the night," the quotation beneath began. Ellen dropped the book on the floor.

The sound was muffled by the rug, yet it brought her mother. She stopped at the edge of the room. "Who—?"

Ellen stepped out from behind the bed curtain. "I was looking at Susie in the yearbook."

Mrs. Cage gasped and began to pant. Sweat stood out on her forehead. "That picture, yes, I remember, it's very pretty. I never noticed before how much you look like it."

"Like it or like her?"

"Like her." Mrs. Cage dabbed her forehead. "You've always looked like her, only you wouldn't believe it."

"Maybe I'll believe it now you've told me. I've always wanted to believe I looked like her."

"I don't know anything about you, anything at all," her mother said.

For a moment, the silence between them seemed about to burst into laughter or screams. Then Mrs. Cage said, "I have to get back to deal with those notes. I'm making a list of names and addresses so I'll be ready when the engraved cards come."

She turned briskly toward her room. Ellen trailed behind.

Mrs. Cage sat down at her desk and picked up a fresh sheet of paper. "People are so kind. Of course, they don't think of the trouble it causes. I've already written down forty-seven names; it'll take me the rest of the summer to get them all answered."

Ellen sat down on the foot of the chaise longue. Her mother's white bed jacket, embroidered with flowers, slipped to the floor, and she picked it up and laid it carefully across her lap. "I was just wondering how Susie seemed to you, the last time you saw her."

"In June?" Mrs. Cage looked at her warily. "I went up then to get her settled at Mrs. Chrysler's. She didn't have any summer clothes, so we went into the little town and found a nice shop; she got some lovely things. A beige silk suit, I remember. She seemed fine, Ellen."

"And between June and now you had her letters."

"Yes. They are really marvelous. I've saved them—you might like to see."

"I don't want to see." Ellen felt as though she were going to choke, and she stood up quickly, letting go of the bed jacket. When she saw it lying crumpled on the floor, she picked it up and spread it on the chaise longue. "Letters don't mean anything," she said.

"Then what does mean anything?" Her mother looked at her, poised, her pen in her hand.

"None of this stuff, none of what you're doing," Ellen said, and began to cry; her mouth gaped like a fish.

"Poor darling," her mother said. "Would you like one of these?" She picked up a pill bottle from the corner of the desk.

"No!"

"Well, I know I couldn't have gotten through without them," Mrs. Cage said, replacing the bottle.

"Is it through already?"

"No. It's just beginning. There will be many more people to deal with tomorrow, when the aunts and the cousins come."

"I mean, is she through? Is nobody ever going to know any more about her?"

"Ellen, my dear, if you really want to do something, you should go down and help Art. He's running back and forth like a chicken with its head off. You take the back door."

"I refuse to," she said.

Her mother shook her head. "Thirty-two years old and still an adolescent," she said. "Don't you know there's nothing else you can do?"

"Then I might as well leave."

"That I won't allow. We all have to go through this together."

Mrs. Cage turned back to her desk and bent her head. Ellen saw the nape of her neck flash, like a piece of silver.

She turned and went out of the room. At the top of the stairs, she stopped, listening to the noise below. The telephone was ringing, unanswered. Then the doorbell pierced through and she heard Art's voice: ". . . so very kind." Someone was leaving something. The descent to the hall below seemed suddenly very long, and she imagined rolling as Susan had rolled into the grinding waves, which must have seemed to her as soft as velvet.

of groceries. Hearing her crash around the kitchen, Jake knew that the subway, the wind, and the crowd at the market had revived all her resentments. She wanted to leave her job, and it was only with great effort that he had persuaded her to stay on a little longer. She would be miserable at home. The refrigerator door banged and there was a clatter of cans in the closet. "We've got that party at the Dawsons' tonight," he called.

She did not answer, and the sounds of her beleaguered domesticity grew louder. Finally she came into the bathroom and look[ed] at Jake, lying afloat in the tub.

"I thou[ght] we'd eat out," he said, sitting up and pulling the plug.

"On w[hat?]" As he stood up, she transferred her pale stare to the tile[ ].

"I got a[ ] cashed this morning."

"That [ ]he account is overdrawn again."

He rea[ched] st her for the towel. "Only till Friday. They won't car[e] call I'll tell them it's coming."

She pu[t]e against his face before he could dry it. After a m[ ] kissed her but her mouth was dry and unrelenting. [ ]toned her stiff white blouse and kissed her breasts an[d]d her back, sighing with relief.

As he b[ ] up again, Jake's fingers began to tremble. The tiny [ ]er neck, [ ]e his hands feel swollen and the curve of [ ] He turned[ ]lnerable, ravished him with tenderness. [ ]d up h[ ]g the little buttons, which she quickly [ ]d went[ ] wrapped the towel around his waist [ ]ge acts[ ] room to get a drink. None of her [ ]d him [ ] but sometimes a gesture, a detail, [ ]rmons,[ ]ught. He was not bothered by her [ ] of liv[ ]d them: "I'm sick of working, I'm [ ] left a[ ]al life going to begin?" But when [ ]ry on[ ]s path or spread her underpants [ ]was to[ ]ed and pushed back her hair— [ ]he to[ ]im with her ordinariness. [ ]could which even in the best of times [ ]was pleased. Expanding in her

THE FACTS OF HIS LIFE

Several times that winter, Jake found himself wondering how he had arrived at the position he was in: his New York life, paid for by his wife's job, his half-finished novel, his affair with Myra Long. He knew that he had not chosen any of it. Yet he was defined by his situation as he had never expected to be, for the facts of his life had seemed when he was younger as irrelevant as the facts on his driver's license. But now when he thought of the effort he would have to make to change any of it, he felt nearly helpless. He was only twenty-seven and his life was as settled as a suburban housewife's, doing her laundry on the same day every week.

To comfort himself, he went for long walks every afternoon, searching the faces of passersby for their opinion. They did not seem to notice him as much as they once had when their faces, strangers and friends alike, had reflected some of the magic he had felt in himself. He had been so bright at school; he had stunned his parents and his teachers with his brashness, his certainty of success. Other people still saw that, at times; old friends still came to him for energy and advice. But the ladies walking dogs in the park did not see it and were no longer startled by his intense staring eyes.

He always stopped at Sixty-seventh Street to look at the soldiers on the war monument. Their metal faces seemed as beautiful to him as trees or stones, free of the distortions of conflict and choice. He imagined climbing up among them and being absorbed into the simple fury of their charge, and one day when he saw a little boy sitting there, casually, on a metal knee, he stood amazed as though once again anything were possible.

Late in January, he came back from his walk gnawed to the bone by the cold. The heat in his apartment building made his head buzz, and his fingers—he never wore gloves—felt swollen and coarse. He had not worked all day and the hours wasted lay across him like an iron belt.

As he unlocked the door to his apartment, he heard the telephone ringing. He went slowly to answer it, closing the door first and dropping off his coat yet all the time drawn through the little interconnecting rooms to the telephone, which sat in a pile of papers beside his bed. He knew who was calling. Even the ring had her persistence, her calm continual pattern.

"Yes," he said as he picked up the receiver and continued to get out of his clothes.

"I just wanted to tell you . . . how sorry I am about lunch, the way I acted." Myra's voice faded and then surged back into his ear.

"I'm sorry, too."

"I didn't want to make a scene. That's the last thing I wanted to do. But you seemed so far away, after yesterday."

"I always seem far away to you, after yesterday."

"Yes." In a while he began to hear her breathing, little labored pants like a small animal run almost off its legs. She breathed like that when they were in bed together, prostrated even by her pleasures. "Jake?"

"Yes?"

"What are you doing right now?"

"I'm taking off my clothes."

"Oh!" she said with appetite.

"I'm going to take a bath!" he yelped, and then he had to laugh.

She laughed too. "We are a pair of fools."

"I wouldn't say a pair." Her humor made him generous. "You want a lot, you've been through a lot. It's time for your reward, your chocolate cake."

"I don't like chocolate," she murmured. "But when I was

---

away, your letters . . . I thought you w

"You were lonely, Myra." After six m had gone away for her divorce, but the Reno had weakened her resolution. Thre to ask Jake to join her. He had been te degree. His life without her had been bl pected, his days had seemed long, and in sat with his wife, absorbed yet with a str ment.

"The trouble is, I made that decision b said.

"I know. I warned you about that, bu sure."

"The spirit is willing but the flesh is weak

"Look, I've got to hang up. Maryann minute and we've got to go out."

"Party?" she asked and Jake thought set with a pathetic attempt at style on a

"Yes. I wish I could ask you to come. There was a soft pause.

"I need a life of my own!" she sh ear.

Unable to agree entirely, he

"Why don't you come by toni

"Because I'll be with Marya

"Why do I offer," she mou

"Good-by," he said and h

He went on lethargicall to sleep with Myra; he the beginning. He had her revelations, used who was one of his naked body had str pared for the me the tiny depresse but naked she

While he

THE FACTS OF HIS LIFE

Several times that winter, Jake found himself wondering how he had arrived at the position he was in: his New York life, paid for by his wife's job, his half-finished novel, his affair with Myra Long. He knew that he had not chosen any of it. Yet he was defined by his situation as he had never expected to be, for the facts of his life had seemed when he was younger as irrelevant as the facts on his driver's license. But now when he thought of the effort he would have to make to change any of it, he felt nearly helpless. He was only twenty-seven and his life was as settled as a suburban housewife's, doing her laundry on the same day every week.

To comfort himself, he went for long walks every afternoon, searching the faces of passersby for their opinion. They did not seem to notice him as much as they once had when their faces, strangers and friends alike, had reflected some of the magic he had felt in himself. He had been so bright at school; he had stunned his parents and his teachers with his brashness, his certainty of success. Other people still saw that, at times; old friends still came to him for energy and advice. But the ladies walking dogs in the park did not see it and were no longer startled by his intense staring eyes.

He always stopped at Sixty-seventh Street to look at the soldiers on the war monument. Their metal faces seemed as beautiful to him as trees or stones, free of the distortions of conflict and choice. He imagined climbing up among them and being absorbed into the simple fury of their charge, and one day when he saw a little boy sitting there, casually, on a metal knee, he stood amazed as though once again anything were possible.

Late in January, he came back from his walk gnawed to the bone by the cold. The heat in his apartment building made his head buzz, and his fingers—he never wore gloves—felt swollen and coarse. He had not worked all day and the hours wasted lay across him like an iron belt.

As he unlocked the door to his apartment, he heard the telephone ringing. He went slowly to answer it, closing the door first and dropping off his coat yet all the time drawn through the little interconnecting rooms to the telephone, which sat in a pile of papers beside his bed. He knew who was calling. Even the ring had her persistence, her calm continual pattern.

"Yes," he said as he picked up the receiver and continued to get out of his clothes.

"I just wanted to tell you . . . how sorry I am about lunch, the way I acted." Myra's voice faded and then surged back into his ear.

"I'm sorry, too."

"I didn't want to make a scene. That's the last thing I wanted to do. But you seemed so far away, after yesterday."

"I always seem far away to you, after yesterday."

"Yes." In a while he began to hear her breathing, little labored pants like a small animal run almost off its legs. She breathed like that when they were in bed together, prostrated even by her pleasures. "Jake?"

"Yes?"

"What are you doing right now?"

"I'm taking off my clothes."

"Oh!" she said with appetite.

"I'm going to take a bath!" he yelped, and then he had to laugh.

She laughed too. "We are a pair of fools."

"I wouldn't say a pair." Her humor made him generous. "You want a lot, you've been through a lot. It's time for your reward, your chocolate cake."

"I don't like chocolate," she murmured. "But when I was

away, your letters . . . I thought you were saying something."

"You were lonely, Myra." After six months of discussion, she had gone away for her divorce, but the time she had spent in Reno had weakened her resolution. Three times, she had called to ask Jake to join her. He had been tempted to a surprising degree. His life without her had been bleaker than he had expected, his days had seemed long, and in the evenings he had sat with his wife, absorbed yet with a strange quiver of resentment.

"The trouble is, I made that decision because of you," Myra said.

"I know. I warned you about that, but you said you were sure."

"The spirit is willing but the flesh is weak."

"Look, I've got to hang up. Maryann will be home in a minute and we've got to go out."

"Party?" she asked and Jake thought of her cheese sandwich set with a pathetic attempt at style on a porcelain plate.

"Yes. I wish I could ask you to come."

There was a soft pause.

"I need a life of my own!" she shouted suddenly, close to his ear.

Unable to agree entirely, he said, "I'll call you tomorrow."

"Why don't you come by tonight, after the party?"

"Because I'll be with Maryann."

"Why do I offer," she mourned to herself.

"Good-by," he said and hung up exhausted.

He went on lethargically undressing. It had not been his idea to sleep with Myra; he had recognized the threat in that from the beginning. He had been used to dealing with her tears and her revelations, used even to advising her about her husband, who was one of his oldest and best-cherished friends; but Myra's naked body had struck him a secret blow. He had not been prepared for the meagerness: the knobbed knees, the sharp hips, the tiny depressed breasts. Dressed, she was an unhappy woman, but naked she had the advantages of a starving child.

While he was bathing, Maryann came in with an armload

of groceries. Hearing her crash around the kitchen, Jake knew that the subway, the wind, and the crowd at the market had revived all her resentments. She wanted to leave her job, and it was only with great effort that he had persuaded her to stay on a little longer. She would be miserable at home. The refrigerator door banged and there was a clatter of cans in the closet. "We've got that party at the Dawsons' tonight," he called.

She did not answer, and the sounds of her beleaguered domesticity grew louder. Finally she came into the bathroom and looked at Jake, lying afloat in the tub.

"I thought we'd eat out," he said, sitting up and pulling the plug.

"On what?" As he stood up, she transferred her pale stare to the tiles.

"I got a check cashed this morning."

"That means the account is overdrawn again."

He reached past her for the towel. "Only till Friday. They won't care. If they call I'll tell them it's coming."

She put her face against his face before he could dry it. After a minute he kissed her but her mouth was dry and unrelenting. He unbuttoned her stiff white blouse and kissed her breasts and she arched her back, sighing with relief.

As he buttoned her up again, Jake's fingers began to tremble. The tiny buttons made his hands feel swollen and the curve of her neck, drooping, vulnerable, ravished him with tenderness. He turned away, cursing the little buttons, which she quickly did up herself. Then he wrapped the towel around his waist and went into the living room to get a drink. None of her large acts threatened him but sometimes a gesture, a detail, laid him bare to an onslaught. He was not bothered by her "sermons," as they both called them: "I'm sick of working, I'm sick of living; when is my real life going to begin?" But when she left a runover shoe in his path or spread her underpants to dry on the radiator or sighed and pushed back her hair— that was too much; she pierced him with her ordinariness.

So he took her to a restaurant which even in the best of times they could not afford. Maryann was pleased. Expanding in her warmth, Jake ordered a whole bottle of wine and afterward, a brandy. Maryann asked for a cigar and lighted it and leaned back with the nearly real elegance Jake had always prized. A man at the next table turned to stare and Jake smiled at him with proprietary courtesy. He would have liked to tell the stranger how pretty and how minor Maryann had been when he first met her; how she had dazzled him with her blood-red tights and her passionate opinions. They had been in college then and they had argued for hours, or rather, he had sat and listened to her railings. He had loved the vigor of her mind even while he had ignored its contents. Later, in his arms, she would recant feverishly. "You know I only say . . . I only want to be what you want." He had thought it wonderful that such intensity could be so swiftly diverted.

After the dinner, the wine, and the brandy, Jake did not have enough money to pay the bill. He asked Maryann for five dollars, which she pressed into his hand, surreptitiously, under the table. They left the restaurant smiling, borne along on the impression they had created.

At the door of the Dawsons' apartment, a maid separated them. Jake was sent to leave his coat in a child's bedroom, and when he came back, his wife had already gone into the party. Jake was disappointed; she must have made a handsome entrance, alone, trailing her mysteries. He hesitated, listening to the boom of conversation in the big room beyond the arch. He could not sort out a word; it was a solid shining wall onto which presently he would cast his shadow. Yet he hesitated, remembering years before when he would have waited indefinitely, hoping for a glance, a sign of recognition to smooth his way in. He had been unknown when he first came to New York and he remembered that from time to time with panic. Finally, aware of the maid watching, he plunged into the crowd and made his way quickly to the bar.

As soon as he had a drink, he began to make his rounds. He knew which people he wanted to talk to and he separated them one by one from their other conversations, listened a moment to their banalities, and then cut through to the core. "I hear

Susan has gone to Riggs," he would say abruptly, or, "What happened about Washington?" He had wanted to speak to Larry Long but as soon as Larry saw him, he left the room. Jake was always hurt by Larry's behavior. They had been friends for years and would continue to be friends when Myra's rage and pain had sunk into the past. Jake went quickly to talk to another old friend who had spent the winter in a haze of emotional problems. As he listened to an account of a hopelessly damaged week, Jake wished he did not have to know so many people so well. Yet it was that or nothing for him; his friends' lives did not offer any superficial connections. Their fringes, their polite personalities, seemed thin and ragged to him. But the core remained hard, obscure, dark, seedy, and more and more protuberant as the petals fell away. Two of the people he approached were naked stamen and pistil, peeled by his perception to the dreadful rudiments.

When he saw Myra waving darkly over the crowd, he turned away, already knowing too much.

He was surprised to see her. She did not often go to parties, having lost since her divorce most of her husband's connections. She looked as dark that night as the eye of a sunflower; each grain of her personality stood out. He recognized her dress—it was one she had bought to please him—and he could not help knowing why she had chosen to wear her coral beads. Oh infinite variety! He had slept with her eleven or twelve times and already she was revealing in the way she had arranged her hair every thought which had passed through her head since their last meeting.

It was merciful that he had never had to live with her. She would have given tongues to her clothes, her dripping stockings would have mourned for him; she would have raised an army against him from the furnishings of her bedroom. Her children made that triumph unlikely; they had been known to invade her bed at five in the morning.

She got him at last with his back to the bar. He had been talking for some time to a sad young girl in purple. As Jake inclined his head to hear her soft complaints, he inhaled her fragrances undivided and shot his glance deep into her round white heart.

And then Myra was at his elbow, flushed, intense, smelling of talcum powder. "Jake?" She rang his name like a clapper. The sad young girl obediently drifted away.

Myra was turning her glass; it squeaked in her damp hand. "What's the matter?" Jake asked, more gently than he had intended. A line of sweat stood out above her thick sweet mouth and he remembered their times together, each small, distinct, and self-contained as a drop of water.

"Larry brought me here," she said at a tangent.

"It's nice of him to bring you to parties."

She would not rise to his irony. "I haven't seen you for so long, I mean really seen you," she said, launching suddenly into the middle of her complaint.

"I've been working."

"Is it going well?" she asked. Jake knew she hoped to find herself one day a dusty precious flower pressed in the pages of his book.

"It's going all right. Look, we did have lunch together."

"Oh, I can't count that—not when I behaved so badly."

"Don't feel so badly about it."

"It doesn't bother you at all?"

"Look, I've got to go and speak to Duncan about his review."

She clutched his arm, nearly dropping her glass. "Jake!" Then picking up brightly as he gave her his attention, she said, "Jake: I think I've fallen in love with you."

He stared at her. "Yes, I love you, too."

"No. I mean the real thing." She spoke as if she were holding it in her hand.

Jake was shocked. He opened his mouth and closed it again. There was really nothing he could say. She had crossed their limits and he felt embarrassed for her.

At the same time he noticed the tip of her ear, dividing her long black hair.

"And I mean to make you fall in love with me," Myra said, laying her hand lightly on the back of his neck.

He was still staring at her ear. He knew her breasts, her thighs, her large hungry demands, but the little end of her ear was new to him. Hardly hearing himself, he said, "I don't really think you want me."

"I don't care what you think," she said staunchly. "I left Larry for you, I went to Reno for you. I'm not going to give up now."

At that Jake was released. He knew what she was saying and he looked at her with his usual concern. "Have you talked this over with Larry?"

"Of course not! Why should I?"

"Because you still depend on his opinion."

"Not to that extent. He would be perfectly furious," she added complacently.

"You see what I mean. You really should discuss this with him."

"But it's you I'm in love with!"

"Yes, but it's you I'm thinking about."

"Don't think about me, I'm fine." Confused, she pressed closer to him. "Say you'll give me a chance."

"Of course I will." Furtively, he was examining her, as though he would be able to detect a further hardening of intent like a bone breaking through her pale skin. "I have to think about you first, that's all," he said. "You know I can't give you anything commensurate."

"Don't say that, Jake."

"You've known that from the start."

"No!"

"I've told you that all along."

"You told me you'd never leave Maryann."

"That, and the other."

"You said something else when you made love to me."

Startled, he rummaged his memory. "I never said—"

"I don't mean words!"

In that crowd, they were attracting no attention; Jake was at one of his usual posts. Yet he glanced around uneasily. Myra's voice was shrill. "Look, I've got to go now," he said, pressing her hand. "I'll see you tomorrow for lunch."

She stepped back. Amazed at the ease, he turned away; and then, behind him, she began to scream.

Jake looked back. She had thrown her chin up, opening her mouth thirstily to the scream; he could see the cords in her long throat. The sound flew up without a quiver, triumphantly sweeping over the heads of the crowd: rage, rage without a tear to bring it down.

Jake hurried away. Out of the corner of his eye, he saw Maryann rushing to Myra and then the scream ceased abruptly, as though something had been crammed down her throat.

He went quickly down the long hall to get his coat, and then he let himself out of the apartment. As he waited for the elevator, he thought how angry Myra would be if she knew that her great outcry had moved him less than the tip of her ear. Her scream lay beyond his hearing, like her solemn listing of complaints, but that little tip of ear had almost finished him. As he stepped into the elevator, he shuddered once, violently. "Cold!" the elevator man exclaimed. "Wind out there like a knife!" But it was the whistle of her single arrow past his head which had made him tremble. Jake knew he could not run that risk again.

If she called in the morning, he would listen to her apologies and then tell her he could not allow her to go on destroying herself. If she called again, he would go to Connecticut for a while. He had been thinking of getting out of town, to finish his novel.

Only the memory of her mouth bothered him and he felt proud and sad as he realized that he would never again allow himself to kiss her.

Fifth Avenue was abandoned, given over to the cold. A taxi cruised by and Jake put his hand in his pocket to see if he could muster the fare. He had a quarter and he thought of brazening his way home on that, but he felt too tender for another human contact. He put his hands in his pockets and walked quickly up the street.

The monument at Sixty-seventh Street loomed out of the darkness, glittering under its bank of lights. Jake stopped in front of it. On one side of the pedestal, a dying soldier sagged in a comrade's arms. Jake stared at the boy's face, blind, anonymous, ennobled by the final loss of will. Tears came into his eyes, for himself still fighting these Indian wars as well as for the dying metal soldier. They were both engaged in mortal combat, both defiant and doomed. Jake raised his hand, saluting his comrade, his forerunner, and then went on quickly up the avenue.

THE BIG DAY

Their parents had told them, at one time or another, that it would be better for them to wait and get married after Jeffrey's tour of duty was over, and they had agreed, without going into it, that this was what they were going to do. They were used to waiting. During college, they had waited almost five months before sleeping together, in order to be sure that it was the right thing for them, and after that, they had waited a year before deciding that they wanted to marry. For Jeffrey, the waiting seemed to put an edge on the final satisfaction; Ann remembered how he had sat up in bed to exclaim, "At last! At last!" He was proud, too, that they could be so sensible about their decision to marry; it seemed to add to their maturity. None of the grownups had been able to say that they were too young, although they were both just out of college. "We thought about it for fifty-two weeks," Jeffrey had told them. And then, of course, he would be away for eighteen months before their decision could take.

Yet as the time grew closer, Ann noticed that he was losing confidence. He asked her several times what she would do about other men while he was gone, and she found it rather hard to convince him—for it was all so out of range—that she would never notice other men at all. It was true that she never noticed them now; Jeffrey was always with her, talking, looking, his face planted so firmly in her attention that even when she was alone, she found herself composing conversations with him. She had grown up very much on her own, without brothers or sisters or close friends, and Jeffrey filled a space which had been there for so long she had not known it was there, until he occupied it. "I'll have your letters, after all," she told him. "And the job will keep me busy."

He turned on her at that with a flash of irritation. "I didn't know your job was going to be so important."

"It's just the same old job," she reminded him; he was used to her complaints about the boredom and senselessness of working in the college library.

"Yes, but there'll be people around," he said somberly. "All those goons, taking books out." Her job was to bring books down from the stacks, and she and Jeffrey had laughed over the looks she received when she arrived to deliver her armful. She was a pretty girl, and there was something pleasantly servile about her job, which made men want to know her.

"Don't you want me to see anybody at all?" she asked.

"Not at night," he said. "Promise me you won't see anyone at night." Suddenly he seemed on the verge of tears. When she went to him and touched his shoulder, he jerked away. "I'll be all right, don't worry," he said grimly.

She knew that he was afraid to go, and although she did not dread it in the same way, she wanted him to leave assured and confident. It would be harder for her to wait if he went off uncertain; that would seem to put the future in jeopardy. She knew her only chance of getting through the time lay in taking the future entirely for granted. There could not be any question: they were going to be married, they were as good as married already. For the first time, she wondered why they were waiting.

"Why don't we get married now?" she asked.

He looked at her, amazed. "But we told them we would wait!"

"We could tell them differently."

"There isn't time, now. I'm going in nine days. How could your mother get everything ready?"

"She doesn't need to. We can just go to a justice of the

peace." She smiled at that. It would be the first rakish thing they had ever done.

"You mean across the river?" He was still aghast.

"Yes, in Indiana, like all the bad people used to do when we were kids."

It took him a while to realize that she was serious, and then he pounced on the idea. She had thought to wait a week, at least, but he saw no reason not to drive to Indiana the next day. He called her mother in and announced their decision with such firmness that Mrs. Stouffer could only gasp. She went upstairs with Ann to look over her dresses for something suitable. Standing in the closet, she glanced back at her daughter. "Honey, are you sure this is the right thing? You two have always been so sensible, I don't like to act like—"

"It's what he wants, Mama."

Mrs. Stouffer sighed. She seemed to be heavy with unspoken words. "Look, here's your navy cotton, it's still practically new. How would that be? Oh, I did want a real wedding!"

"It's the war," Ann said, to take the pressure off her feelings, but she was not sure that was the reason.

They drove across the bridge at eleven the next morning, with Ann's parents and Jeffrey's mother wedged into the back seat. Both the women were wearing small hats, and when Jeffrey rolled down his window, there was a cry from the back. The justice lived in a clapboard house at the end of a narrow street; a neon sign, switched off in daylight, advertised his services. They went inside, shook hands, and took their places. It was over in seven minutes.

Afterward, Ann's parents took everyone to lunch at the big new motel which had been opened on the edge of town. Ann's mother sighed a good deal during lunch, but no one referred to the change of plans. When Jeffrey's mother stood up to make a toast, her voice quavered with what seemed to be pride. "They take on everything, these young people, they don't even have time to be children," she said. The couple at the next table applauded softly. Ann and Jeffrey sat, hands linked, eating a little and waiting for it to be over.

Ann had bought a new nightgown for their first whole night together, even though it had to be in Jeffrey's room, as always; at least this time, his mother had gone to visit her sister. Ann had looked at pastel nightgowns and black nightgowns, but in the end, she had seized a white. They both laughed at that, sitting up in bed the next morning. It was the first time Ann had used her mother-in-law's kitchen to make breakfast, and she found that almost more affecting than anything else. In the old days, she had been obliged to slip out of the house before daylight, to go home and sleep and then eat her bowl of cereal.

Since they could not actually live in Jeffrey's room, Ann found herself spending the days that remained almost exactly as she had before. Only the mornings were different; she and Jeffrey had their breakfast together at the card table in the living room while Mrs. Anderson sat in the kitchen, drinking coffee and listening to the radio. They talked in subdued voices and sometimes held hands until it was late and Ann jumped up to leave. Jeffrey would see her out. She hated to close the screen door behind her because it seemed to shut him in a cage; looking back, she would see the sad white oblong of his face. Once, when it was raining, he rushed out after her with an umbrella. From the bus, she saw him running back up the sidewalk, huddled, already soaked.

On their last morning, Jeffrey woke up before dawn and woke her too, sobbing in the dark. "I'm afraid to leave you alone," he said. "Promise me you'll wait." As she comforted him, holding his big head on her shoulder, Ann felt for the first time that she was not going to be able to stand it. He was piling something heavy on her, a great load of expectations, as though she were going to have to be responsible for living for him, living exactly as he would wish, during the whole time he was away. She wanted to ask him what she should do if he was killed, but she was afraid to say anything at all. There was something harsh in her which she was afraid he would hear; harsh and angry and terribly unsuitable.

Later, at the induction center, where she had to leave him,

she could not cry at all. There was something so preposterous, so unbelievable about the whole thing. She had never left him anywhere before, except at the barbershop. They had planned everything, they had been so careful about each detail of their lives, and now here they were, blundering apart as though none of it mattered. He looked bunched up in his new uniform, the belt cutting him in two; she was glad she would not have to see him after they had shaved off his hair. She wanted it to be over quickly, and although she clung to his shoulders, she felt as though she were pushing him away. He had tears in his eyes and he blinked and blinked, smiling at her, telling her to be brave. Wait! Wait! Wait! She wanted to scream as she turned and walked slowly and calmly down the steps. I'm sick of waiting! When is it going to begin?

Her mother was sitting on the porch when she came home, with a pitcher of iced tea and some molasses cookies. "That's my brave girl," she said tremulously when she saw Ann coming up the walk.

"What's brave about me?" Ann asked savagely.

"Oh, poor child, it's just too much," her mother said, breaking into tears. Ann went straight past her, up to her room, and closed the door with a neat tight click. As she closed it, she imagined slamming it hard, so hard the plaster above the door frame would crack and the glass would shatter in the opposite window, tumbling out onto the white and pink petunias at the edge of the yard.

Next day, she went back to work. The fall term was beginning and she was kept quite busy, going up and down for books. She kept a handkerchief in her pocket, and after she had delivered an order she would turn away, wiping the dust off the tips of her fingers. After a week, she was no longer angry, and she went from her house to the library, to the cafeteria where she ate her lunch, back to the library, and finally home, walking with small quiet steps and a steady face. People treated her as though she were a widow already, stepping aside for her in the street and shining on her with false smiles; the head librarian, particularly, could not do enough for her, and Ann began to hate the woman's kindness. She started wearing her brightest dresses to work, although the heat and the dust of the stacks made them most inappropriate; it seemed to her that the librarian was surprised.

Then Jeffrey's letters began to arrive, every other day, in fat envelopes. Since she did not want to read them in front of her mother, Ann brought them to work and read them in the stacks. The librarian saw her once there and seemed pleased. "The blessing of the mail!" she cried. After that, Ann read his letters at lunch, spreading the thin sheets out next to her plate. They were very long letters and sometimes, when she was in a rush, she would skip a page; that did not seem to alter the meaning of what came before and after. He was so sad and so lonely and so worried about her that he seemed to be writing from a vacuum. She wished that he would give her more details; she was finding it impossible to imagine his days. Instead, he spent paragraphs telling her when she should mail her letters in order to reach him at a certain time, and reminding her to number each one so that he would know if he missed one. At night, when she sat down to write to him, she felt pressed and squeezed, trapped by the words, and it was hard to find anything to write except the same things he wrote: that life was impossible and would go on being impossible until he came back.

Yet the time passed, neither rapidly nor slowly but at its usual dogged pace. In October, her mother gathered red leaves and Ann helped her to dip them in paraffin; they decorated the corner of the living room until it was time to put up the Christmas tree. Jeffrey sent her a little gold brooch for Christmas, with apologies for its size; he had not been able to find the shop in Saigon where he had hoped to buy something more splendid. The people, he said, were unhelpful and strange and he was spending most of his off-duty time in the base library. Next day, Ann pinned the brooch to the corner of her collar when she was dressing to go to the library. Looking at herself in the mirror, she thought she would be mistaken for a school-teacher, a sad left-over woman, and she decided it must be the tiny neat brooch. She took it off and put it in her pocket.

The long winter curved down into April; Ann helped her mother gather pussy willows and then watched the gray buds shred as the shoots emerged, spoiling the arrangement. In May, she had lunch with a girl she had known in school; Minnie brought a folding sun reflector to the cafeteria and sat afterward on the bench outside the library, holding the reflector spread out under her chin. Ann thought she looked ridiculous. "You should take better care of yourself," Minnie said, sideways, but Ann did not answer. She was taking the best care she knew how: filing her nails, washing her hair, eating whole-wheat bread, and weighing herself without fail on Tuesdays. She had lived like that always, always, nothing had changed, except that she was married now and people looked at her.

She had only one wish, as the hot weather began, and that was to become invisible: to move slowly and quietly along her routes, free of pity and surmise. Yet she knew that she was becoming more conspicuous all the time. Her bare arms, in summer dresses, seemed to flash, and her hair, bleached by the sun, was a beacon for strangers, signaling wildly above her placid face.

"Is that hair real?" someone asked her one hot day, in the cafeteria line. When she turned to answer, she saw that it was a boy she had known in high school. She had not spoken three words to him since.

"Oh, Ann, I didn't recognize you from the back," he said casually, passing on down the line with his tray.

As she took a plate of tossed salad, Ann imagined having answered him with something pert: "As real as you are," something like that. He might have laughed then and stayed to chat. Passing the cash register, she saw him at the other end of the room, sitting alone, reading the newspaper. On an impulse, she went toward him. "Do you mind?" she asked, poised above him with her tray.

"Of course not," he said, moving things out of the way and folding his paper down onto his knee. "What do you hear from Jeffrey?" he asked as she arranged her silver.

"Oh, nothing much," she answered. "The war is always the same, if you know what I mean."

He nodded seriously. "When's he getting out?"

"Six more months and I forget how many days."

"That's going to be a big day for you."

"Yes, it will be," she said quietly. He finished his lunch before she did and excused himself, glancing back once nervously. She believed that she had looked very hungry for him and she was ashamed and at the same time exhilarated. He should know what it is to wait! She began to think of him as she was going home that night and, later, in bed. He seemed more real to her than anyone else because she knew so little about him, and she imagined his hands grasping her waist. Twisting away, she got out of bed and went into the bathroom to splash her face with water.

"Six more months!" her mother said, next morning.

As the time dwindled, the two families drew close around her, hedging her in with affection and advice. Her father took her aside one chilly evening to warn her that Jeffrey might seem different after all the time that had passed. She should allow herself a while to get adjusted. Ann nodded, looking at the porch light, which for the first time had not attracted a cluster of moths.

At Christmas, Jeffrey sent her a special letter with a poem he had written. It was called "Ann." The first line read, "Eyes blue as the inland seas." She did not know what seas he was thinking of, and she found it difficult to read the rest. He had never written a poem for her before.

"Next Christmas will be your first Christmas together," her mother said when they were dismantling the tree.

Spring came late that year, and by the end of March, time had slowed down to a steady crawl. The pussy willows were buried under a late snow, and Ann's spring dresses still hung in the closet in a long plastic bag. There was nothing to mark the passing of time, except the things people said to her. "Not long now!" the head librarian remarked, once a week, with sparkling eyes. "What about buying some new dresses?" her father asked, taking bills out of his pockets one Saturday morning. "I guess this will be our last lunch for a while," Minnie said, the following week. Ann wanted to ask what she might be expected to do instead, but she was embarrassed to admit that she did not know. They were all prepared for Jeffrey's return, but Ann did not know what to do to get ready. She had looked several times at her bed and thought that presently she would not sleep there, and she had packed a box of clothes to take over to Jeffrey's house. Beyond that, there was nothing she could think of that would prepare her for his arrival. Her mother told her to have a permanent, but Ann thought it might be better to leave her hair as it had always been. "But you won't want to roll it up at night, now," her mother reminded her. Ann looked at the pink curlers that night, felt them and turned them over, weighing them in her hands like jewels. Everyone was looking at her as though she should be feeling the crest of the wave, feeling the surge of water lifting her up and carrying her toward him, but she did not feel anything at all. On her last day at work, the librarian gave her a box with two pairs of stockings in it. "I wanted to give you something you could use," she said, with a strange twinkle. Ann did not want to leave work, and as she stood holding the box she began, for the first time in months, to cry. The librarian stepped around the edge of her desk and held her against her musty yellow blouse. "Too much strain," she said.

Out of consideration, Ann's parents told her that they would not go with her to the airport to meet Jeffrey's plane. His mother, abashed, asked Ann if she would mind if she went along, and Ann wondered why they were all deferring to her. She had not really planned the day and it would have suited her to wait at home until Jeffrey came to get her. Instead, she and her mother-in-law drove in a taxi to the airport.

The plane was delayed and they went into the grill to have

some lemonade. Mrs. Anderson was wearing a new hat with a bunch of red cherries at the brim; one of the cherries, partially detached, dipped down toward the glass when she drank. "What a pretty outfit!" she had exclaimed when Ann got into the taxi, and Ann had explained that she was wearing the same dress she had worn the day Jeffrey left. It pinched a little at the waist, and she knew she had gained two pounds. "He'll appreciate that," Mrs. Anderson assured her. Ann wanted to tell her that was not the reason she had gained weight, but like everything else she could think of to say, it would be both rude and pointless. She felt as though she were beginning to hate this kindly woman with her gentleness, her useful chatter, and shocked, she curled her hands into fists.

A few minutes later, she stood behind the barricade and watched Jeffrey coming toward her, carrying a little bag and his cap. His dark hair was cut so close that she could see the gray of his scalp, and that made his face look peculiar. Mrs. Anderson sobbed and kissed him, reaching high to grasp his neck; Ann went on looking at him over his mother's shoulder. Smile, she told herself, but her mouth remained fixed. "Hello, Ann," he said huskily and took her in his arms and kissed her cheek. His smell was entirely strange to her, clean and mechanical. She drew back to look at him and he kissed her mouth, pressing his lips tightly against hers. Ann saw his mother, still sobbing and smiling, around the edge of his face.

In the taxi, they sat in silence, side by side in the back seat. Jeffrey reached out suddenly and seized her hand; Ann let it lie in his grasp, which was firm and slightly damp. She wanted to ask him what good it had done for them to wait, what use it had served for them to have been, always, so careful. She thought he might agree with her that there had been no use in it at all, that they had been deceived, like children. They could have cried together then, or screamed. But she did not know how to begin. To fill the gap, his mother began to talk. She told Jeffrey how hard Ann had been working, never missing a day at the library; now it was really time for her to take a rest. "And who knows, maybe she'll have something else to keep her busy before too long!" she cried. Then, ashamed of the intrusion, she sank back into her corner. Jeffrey and Ann went on in their silence, sitting with their hands and elbows welded together. Through his khaki trousers, Ann could feel his thigh, strangely stiff and hard, like a piece of wood.

Mrs. Anderson had already cooked supper and set the table; the food was in the oven, keeping warm. As soon as she had seen them inside the house, she turned to go out again. "I'm going over to visit Louise," she announced. "You two settle down and eat when you're ready." She went out of the door briskly, without a backward look. Ann knew the effort it cost her.

She stood facing Jeffrey in the living room. He had set the small bag down between his feet and he was turning the cap on his hands. "You look fine, Ann, I don't know what she was talking about," he said. "You don't look tired at all."

"She's cooked a big meal, chicken, potatoes, I don't know what. Shall I get it out now?"

"Well, not right this minute. Let's sit down and talk a minute, first." He sat on the couch, tentatively, leaning forward with his hands on his knees.

Ann did not move. "I'm afraid it won't be much good if we leave it in the oven. The chicken'll dry out."

"Come here and talk to me. We haven't said a word yet." He reached out and caught hold of her hands, hanging limply by her sides. He drew her toward him slowly. She sat on his knees, very straight, patting her light dress down.

"I missed you so much," he said, bending his head to kiss her.

"I missed you, too. Letters are awful."

"They don't tell anything. I had the feeling I was writing to ten people at once."

He folded his arms firmly around her and kissed her neck. Ann wanted to struggle. "Shall I get dinner now?"

"We'll eat later, honey," he said with authority. "I didn't come home to eat chicken." He began to unbutton the back of her dress, and she remembered that before when he had done that, she had reached back to help him. Now she sat still, her hands pressing her knees. When he stood up, she slipped off his lap and followed, led by the hand. It seemed to her that she had never had any choice, and her body felt stiff under his fingers. She wondered why he could not leave her alone for a while, give her a chance to get adjusted, and then she wondered whether it was ever going to be possible for her to adjust to his strange wooden ways.

"I kept my promise," he said later, lying on his back, looking up at the ceiling.

She sat up and fastened the hook on her bra. It was not clear to her what promise he meant.

THE WEDDING

On the way to New Jersey, Clare said she felt like throwing up and because he had been putting up with her for eleven months, Tom told her to go ahead.

She rolled down her window and put her head out, and the warm wind tipped off her hat and rolled it on the floor.

"I can't, now," she said after a minute and rolled the window up. "It's gone." She sat looking disconsolate, her hands folded in her lap.

"Your hat's on the floor," Tom said, already sorry he hadn't had the grace to stop the car.

She leaned down with her familiar swooping gesture, so sweet, somehow, nearly saccharine, as though she were scooping fledglings out of their nest; her way with newspapers, flowers, and waste baskets, an enthusiasm out of all proportion which usually turned at once to acrimony or tears. She set the hat straight on her head, like a platter.

"Look in the mirror." He tilted the rear-view mirror toward her, would have taken her shoulder and tilted her toward the mirror if he could have stopped the car. Already her sweetness had soured and she stared at him balefully. "You think I don't know how I look."

"You know and I care," he said, distracted by her harshness.

"You care," she announced, beginning her sermon, "because you're afraid I'll offend. . . ." He did not hear any more for a moment, his eyes fixed on a large airlines billboard beside the highway. The painted plane, winging south, had sunlight along its wings, yellow as honey. "I wish I'd come in my nightgown," Clare was saying.

"That wouldn't have offended them," he said, trying his mild humor, and realized at the same time, as so often happened now, that what he was saying was true: she was so pretty, wrecked, so bruised and appetizing, like a slightly overripe peach.

She reached up, flattered, he didn't know by what, and settled her hat at an appropriate angle on her head. "I hate your uncle," she chanted, "I hate your aunt and your cousins, every one of them. I hate the bride most of all."

"She's not a bride yet."

"I wish I could put a curse on her."

"You used to like her." He couldn't remember how long ago that had been; his cousin's personality had faded for him, too, becoming The Bride as soon as Clare started to call her that. How strange, how maddening, even, that Clare's peculiar point of view should have begun to bleed into his mind. He had held off, for a while; her doctor's diagnosis made her seem remote and nearly safe. But after a while, her weirdness, so pleasant, so charming at times, had seemed to dress up his plain life, turning the subway stanchions into calla lilies, the watch shops on Eighty-sixth Street into dens of carnal delight, and the dismal plodding course of life into a calvary. He had to remind himself that she didn't know hot from cold (at her worst) or black from white in order to remember that everything else about her perceptions was unacceptable. Yet he often wondered what difference it made—black or white, the hat flat or angled on her head—and knew, at least for the moment, that it made all the difference in the world. When her hat was flat she looked insane, and it was that look, like the steely rasp in her voice, which no one who cared about her could bear.

"And I hate the bridegroom most of all," she said sullenly, comparing her thumbnails like stamps, side by side.

"You've never even met him."

"I know about him, though. I know what he thinks he's doing." She glared at Tom. "He thinks he's going to start all over again, just go back and start over fresh! He thinks he can just cross out what's already happened."

"I don't know what he thinks."

"I know!" she went on raptly. "I knew as soon as I saw his face!" (When? Tom wondered, and had to take a minute to be sure that Clare had never seen William Borden at all.) "He thinks he can make it that he wasn't married before, he thinks he can just make her disappear—his first wife. He thinks he can even make three children disappear. Quite a magician!" She added with her heavy, dragging irony.

"Aunt Lucy said his first wife was impossible."

She laughed. "Who's possible, I'd like to know? Except you." She turned, grinning, and he felt cold and smiled.

"I do take good care of you, Clare."

She snorted. "And that out there is the garden spot of the world." She gestured at the stinking marshes. "They should lie in those ditches for their honeymoon," she went on thoughtfully.

"Clare, do me a favor, don't say any more till you meet him."

"I'll say enough then," she promised and sang the rest of the way, a droning little song he had never heard before: "Fiddledeedee, Fiddledeedee, the fly has married the bumblebee."

That was what other people could never understand, Tom thought as the song drilled his patience: what it was like to go out with Clare into the world, without protection, never knowing what she might say or do or, which was the worst of all, if she would say or do nothing, simply sitting with her gnomic smile, her chin in her hand, until the sane people around her went mad with effort, aping, wisecracking to break her silence.

Yet Tom had insisted on taking her to the wedding, against everyone's advice; had insisted out of a stubborn refusal to believe that she was really impossible—a refusal he had not even known was there, since he had spent the last eleven months shielding her from every possible group or strain. She had come out of the hospital as fragile as a blown eggshell, and it had never occurred to him before to put her to any kind of test. Yet he had leapt at the wedding. It was as though the smell of stephanotis might bring her back; for she had been glazed and strained at their own wedding, five years before (but not this bad, of course—he would have known) and the flurry of the proceedings had shot her whole into his arms.

Or was it darker than that, his little motivation? He did not like his aunt, who had brought him up as a charity case, he loathed his broad unwieldy uncle, and he had loved their daughter too much, years ago, and been laid bare. Now the occasion would have to be taken seriously. No one who was normal could quibble at that, any more than choke on the imported champagne or vomit up the black Russian caviar.

The gravel in the circular drive whispered under their tires, whispered under the tires of the big car in front of them and sang a little refrain; Tom remembered listening to that lullaby as a child, in a bedroom upstairs, with the headlights wheeling across the walls. The lights and the song had seemed to be life itself, always put off, unapproachable. From the top of the stairs, the grownups in the hall below had looked like big bouquets, a blossom breaking off here or there—a lady in bright colors. It seemed to be their fault that, lately, the colors had faded.

One of the gardener's sons was taking cars but Tom waved him on and drove to the big lawn; he did not want to go inside just yet. The grass was soggy from rain, and he felt the car sink in and knew that next day the lawn would be hopelessly rutted. He had not thought to bring Clare's boots, and he jumped out of the car and went around to lift her over the mud; but she was already out, sinking before he could get to her to the edges of her white sandals. He tried to lift her up in his arms but she laughed and fought free, running with squelching sounds across the grass to the drive. There she consented to wait while he knelt down and cleaned her shoes as best he could with his handkerchief.

They went in hand in hand. The big door was opened by Nelly, his friend from years before, and he was glad to see that Clare remembered her. They walked on through the green-and-gray living room, the walls banked with magnolia, out through the French windows onto the terrace. There were many people gathered there, and Clare's smile was not specific as he introduced her, naming names clearly in the dim hope that she would remember the connections, the details she had once relished. Old Uncle John, the seafaring man with his gold-buttoned blazer and cap, who really could sail and really did know the tides and the winds and yet was a bulbous drunk who put his hand up the parlormaids' skirts. Old Winny, his wife, worn down by trying. Old everyone, Tom realized; they had aged in the year since Clare had been sick, their faces smoothly seamed or powder-caked under the bright lash of the spring sun.

Tulips were leaning out from the borders along the lawn, and he took Clare there for a moment. He had a sense of her limited elasticity which came mainly from her voice, rising so quickly out of the clear registers into the hard grating cry, seagull-like, of her rages. She picked a red tulip and crushed it quickly in her hand, but carefully, holding it out of sight behind her dress. "Pick me a flower," he said, loving her for the childish angry gesture. She picked him another, pinching off the stem so short that the tulip sat like a pair of tongues on the palm of her hand. "When are the real ones coming?" she asked anxiously, and he led her to the bird bath and the altar, banked with smilax and white lilac branches.

Looking back at the terrace, he saw the people gathered there —his friends, his family—like a solid wall.

"What do you think of leaving now, we could drive out to the real country," he muttered, not expecting her to reply.

"But we must see the bride!" she cried, faint and far. "It wouldn't be right to leave without seeing the bride!"

He lost her after that, for a moment, having fallen into conversation with a friend he had not seen since college; not because he was absorbed in what the fellow was saying but because he saw in the smooth declining face the signs of time passing which he had not yet noticed in his own.

Her absence was like a cold breeze; he turned sharply. Aunt Alice, profound in her sense of duty, nodded gravely toward the house. Inside, Nelly, at the door, pointed him toward the downstairs bathroom and he knew from her expression that nothing had gone wrong yet. He stood by the door, his hand on the golden handle, and heard the toilet flushed twice inside.

He opened it cautiously. Clare, her skirts up over her arms, stared at him with fury. "Can't I even—?"

He closed the door and waited. After another interval, afraid that someone was coming, he went quickly in. She was standing in front of the mirror.

"You have no business in here!" she called, her eyes on his reflection.

"Come on out. The service is beginning."

"But I'm pleading," she said.

"Pleading?"

"Bleeding," she pouted. "I didn't know it was time."

He knew from experience where Aunt Alice kept the pads and handed one to her, delicately, in its paper wrapping. He could not look at her, their five years together tearing across in the face of her disappointment; the lost months, the lost years, finally the lost child all washed away on currents of clear bright blood. "Is your dress all right?"

She turned around for him to see, but he could not get his eyes above her ankles, where two sharp bones pointed out, prominent as ears.

Aunt Alice would take her upstairs, he told himself as he lead her out of the bathroom. Aunt Alice would give her something to make her sleep and have Nelly sit with her till arrangements could be made. Aunt Alice would touch his shoulder and murmur something that would, in spite of his ironies, move and console him. The family would fold around him if he could acknowledge his need. It was unthinkable. He took Clare to the terrace, and because the company had moved out to the smilax altar, they came along behind, conspicuously, scuttling ahead of the bridal procession.

Catching Clare's waist, he turned her toward the people coming, remembering how she had loved the pomp and display. The little flower girls, his young cousins, had daisies in their hair and tripped along in agonies of shyness. Behind, two older girls, bowed with large meanings, wore hats whose long streamers floated on the breeze. He was amazed by all their feet, light and quick as petals, and wondered what they felt or if they felt at all. Behind, the real people came marching stiffly, and he touched Clare's waist insistently. But her face was turned, she was nodding and smiling, and he felt her hair touch his shoulder.

"The bride," he pleaded in her ear, for she was nodding at the row of tulips.

She turned, then; he felt her eyes align with his, felt her rigidity as she watched that other girl in white. Cousin Lucy was pretty that day, with the abashed radiance of a flickering light; he had always loved her dovelike uncertainties and was glad to see that her wedding had not reassured her. The flowers in her hands were shaking violently and she clung to her father's arm (he was drunk, and walked mincingly) as though it were a barrier against the flood. She did not dare to move her eyes from the minister's face, drinking his words desperately.

The man, William Borden, detached himself from the crowd and came up front; Tom watched him carefully. He was familiar, in his uniform and his careful self-control; it was difficult to see beyond the reassuring details. Strong staff to weak woman, the boy had laid aside his youth and looked like a seamless grandfather. All his experience was gathered in his round pale face: a lamp to the future. Tom felt a laugh like an itch and at the same time heard Clare laughing; softly, sweetly, like a dinner bell. He felt the quivers in her side and held her fiercely, pressing down the laughter with his arm. Fortunately the minister was possessed of a strong voice and the gentle even laughter was drowned. It was not so easy to disguise the tears which ran smoothly down her cheek; the other eye as far as he could tell was dry.

Someone behind him pressed a handkerchief into his hand; he felt the monogram under his thumb.

At last music rang out from somewhere—trumpeters concealed in the honeysuckle—and the pair marched off to the house. The group broke up in merriment, and Tom thought he heard the same hoarse hysterical cackle in their voices that he had been afraid to hear in Clare's. She was holding the handkerchief to her nose, like a child asked to blow. He took it away and put it in his pocket.

A waiter came to them first of all, and Clare took two glasses of champagne.

"Put that down while you drink the first one," he advised her, but she drank one quickly and poured the other in the tulips.

It was easier, now, to disguise what she was doing; people were moving around freely, talking loudly, drinking, already losing track of what was going on. A tall white wedding cake had made its appearance, and the pair was coming out to cut it with a sword. Clare clapped her hands when she saw the shining blade, drawn with due reverence from its socket. "Oh, he has a sword!" she whispered. The cake was passed on little china plates which Tom remembered from birthday parties. A pink rose lay on his slice and he presented it to Clare and watched her gulp it in one large bite. "I'm hungry," she said, "get me another slice!" While he went quickly to get another, the toasting began.

He saw what she was doing in Willy Morris's eyes as Willy handed him another slice of cake; Willy Morris, who had served cake at birthday parties and had perfected a discreet ambivalent smile. But now his flat dark eyes were full of reflections as he looked over Tom's head, back toward the terrace. Tom did not turn until he had taken a silver fork and felt its coolness in his hand; by then it was too late and he turned, slowly, into the sound of Clare's raised voice.

She was standing on a wicker chair, the seat wavering under her feet, and Tom wondered who in the world had hoisted her up there.

She raised her empty champagne glass in one hand, her eyes on the clouds, her voice floating out in ribbons. "We have come here today to celebrate the feast of marriage," she was singing.

People directly beneath her were watching cautiously, and as she continued, the ones who were farther away turned toward her until finally the whole group on the terrace was facing her, a wheel with her face at the hub.

"And yet the thing is, if we are to be honest and celebrate this thing the way it should be celebrated, the past has to be brought in; I mean, you can't sing to the flower without including the bud and the stem and the root, even, with the mud around it, too. I want to make a toast to William or should I say Bill, whom I don't really know at all: The Bridegroom." Before they could interrupt her with polite enthusiasm, before Tom could believe his relief, she was going on. "And to his first bride who is here today though nameless. To her hopes and her struggles and her tears and her despair. The stem must be recognized. And to the three children who are here today too although nobody knows their names. Children are the roots. Ignore the roots and what do you have. An empty ceremony. To William's children! May they grow up in bliss and sadness and come in the end to speak those things which are not spoken. To them!" She raised her glass and, realizing that it was dry, lost her lilt and hesitated; finally reached down and took the glass from someone's hand and drank it slowly. She was not in the midst of silence for more than ten seconds; then voices went up around her, "To Bill!" and every glass was raised to drown what she had said.

Tom felt his aunt at his shoulder before she spoke.

"Tom, you must . . ."

"I know."

He felt her firm pressure, like a clamp, on his arm.

"I'm taking her home right now."

"If you need any help—"

"I won't need any, Aunt Alice. She's said what she came to say."

He left her to consider whether he had known about it from the beginnng; the glitter of this little triumph faded as he began to make his way to Clare.

She was still on her chair, although everyone had moved off
and left her poised like a garden ornament. He touched her
knee. "Come on."

She looked down at him, dazed, smiling, her eyes so bright
with tears he thought at first she had been laughing.

"Help me down," she said, dropping the glass onto the grass
and then stretching out both hands to be taken.

"We'll start back now and stop on the way to eat. There's
a place off the parkway. . . . It has a garden."

"Too cold for gardens," she murmured as she followed him
across the terrace. He knew that certain people were staring
and raised his head, smiling, wearing their concern like a crown.

It was worth letting her have her way to find her, afterward,
so pliant; he lifted her in his arms across the muddy lawn and
placed her in the car and fastened the seat belt across her lap,
feeling her warm body which was what had first drawn
him to her: her limitless pliancy. Going around, getting in and
starting the motor, he was driven by the sight of her profile, set,
pale, and calm, a disobedient child, a hopelessly naughty child
who tells the truth against all reason. He reached over to pat
her and let his hand slide up her arm, cool and pearly, to the
edge of her embroidered sleeve. "Clare, you really told them."

She looked at him thoughtfully. "I knew him for what he was
from the time we met him at Malibu."

"When?"

"He took me on his lap there on the terrace and kissed my
neck—a white kiss—and said he wanted to tell me about his
troubles. Hypocrite, I said, it won't get you anywhere."

"I don't remember," Tom said dully, dropping his hand from
her arm.

She went on for a little. He watched the road and the even
woods which stretched far enough on each side to hide the
houses; a limitless sense of open country was imposed by that
half acre of spindly trees. The relief of money, its precious
illusions. He thought of moving Clare out here, to a brick
fortress or a Normandy château where her eccentricity could
atrophy slowly and become, like topiary hedges, heated dog

runs, and mahagony stables, simply another attribute of the rich. But he would still have to face her in the morning over coffee or at night when he tried to sleep through her whistlings and moaning—the nightmares that no medication had been able to erase.

Still talking, she moved closer to him and rubbed against his side, her set, rapt face discounting everything she was saying, and her warm arm, hot almost, fresh from the fiery oven, still the pale arm of a little girl who is allowed to make mistakes.

"I want to go to bed with you," she said, hot-eyed.

"Look at me, first." But she wouldn't, her eyes were fixed on the trees.

He wondered who she thought he was and whether he could persuade her to take her tranquilizers; he had them in his pocket and it was only a question of stopping somewhere for a cup of water. Usually he could persuade her to swallow them, especially when he held her in his arms and kissed her first, sliding the pills into her mouth after the kisses, sliding the edge of the paper cup between her lips and then kissing her again, for drinking.

He began to look for a place to stop to get the water. Before the thruway, he remembered, there was a diner. She was against him all the time, her thigh beside his thigh, and in the midst of worrying about her and thinking of the pills, he knew she had sensed his excitement. Bruised, rapt, and silent, she never knew who he was, in bed; her frenzies were mechanical; and yet he wanted her, in spite or because. . . . Because, because . . . It rang in his head, for a moment, that she was mad and he was hopeless; but then he felt the smooth line of her leg, pressing through her filmy skirt, and saw the silver diner shining like a lost star through the trees.

A NEW LIFE

On the third day after the baby was born, the air conditioner in Mina's hospital room began to sing. "Over the seas," it sang in a rich female voice. "Over the seas, over the seas to Ireland." Frightened, Mina stared at the thing, clamped between the jaws of the plate-glass window. Then she got up to look at herself in the mirror and was shocked to see how ugly she had become; her face peered out like a starved tiger's from the tangles of her reddish hair. Do something about yourself, the fierce lecture began. Don't just lie there! Have them come and cut your hair or brush it yourself, at least. The voice was her mother's, but her mother had never spoken to her so savagely; gentle, a little timid, she had seldom done more than glance, weightily, over the barrier between the front and back seats when they were being driven interminably somewhere. "Over the seas," the air conditioner droned like a bee engrossed in a flower. Mina doubted that the song existed, but she knew she was responsible for it because it had aroused the other voice, the voice of the lecturer, and that had always been hers.

She had waked early that morning, before the street lamps were turned off outside her window. Raising the shade, she had looked out at the green shoulders of the park trees, which she had passed so often, blindly. A million small new leaves were fluttering in the morning breeze, and she had felt surrounded by lightly clapping hands. A little later, she had heard her baby cry as he was wheeled to her down the hall, and the new milk had tingled in her breasts, spilling out in two small cloudy drops. For the first time, there were no choices: the baby was hungry and she was there to feed him. She had spent most of her life picking and sorting, trying in anguish to decide what was important, what was at least worth while. She had always been told that the serious things, the work, must be put first, yet she had felt that she was losing everything in the process. With the baby, work was play, the searching, deadly play of his mouth on her nipple. There had been no need to sort and pick, and she had dozed while he fed. The air conditioner's song died down and she heard the voice strike through. Sleeping night and day, it said. Seems to me you've done nothing here but sleep.

That's not true, she answered. I didn't sleep at all. I wouldn't even let them give me Pentothal.

Arguing with the voice never got any further than that: a statement, and an answer. Her conviction wilted in the silence that followed. She was not sorry to find herself fading into agreement. After all, she had grown up with the voice; they had lived together in more or less perfect harmony while the slow scenery of her childhood passed. On the silence of the country house, on the silence that lay between her parents, the voice had struck blow after blow, forging maxims which had seemed both discreet and comforting: Work, learn, be honorable, watch your weight, avoid the fond whims of the flesh; scorn the vicious purple lipstick and the low ideals of the people you find around you. When she went away to college, she had heard, for the first time, the strange clang of it; people there spoke to each other while she spoke in asides, against the clatter in her head. Fortunately, she had met Stephen that first fall and they had spent most of their evenings and all of their weekends together. She had not needed to tell him about the voice because he too had the shining look of someone who is directed from within. Looking back, Mina saw them straight as a pair of candles in the midst of the jungling confusion, the dirt and disorder of their friends. A week after graduation, they had married.

For a while then, Mina had lived in a peaceful gabble of lists and compliments. Eventually that chorus had died down and she had heard her old voice again, ranting on a sharper note. When Stephen came home at night, he would find her standing with something in her hand, a potholder or a book, as though he had interrupted her; she had not dared to tell him that sometimes she had been standing like that for half an hour, listening to the lecturer. She had been afraid that he would be disappointed with her, for, like her parents, he loved her liveliness and efficiency.

When she had become pregnant—passing on, by plan, to the next important task—the voice had taken on a new tone, conspiratorial and wary, as though to guide her through a perilous swamp. She had felt the danger too: she had been nearly overwhelmed by appetite and energy. Once she had sat down in front of a loaf of bread and eaten it, slice by slice, from one end to the other, and all the time, the baby had lunged in her stomach as though it rejoiced. Afterward she had rushed to the scale, but it had failed to register the pound of pleasure. At that moment it had seemed unlikely that she would ever be thin or well disciplined again.

As the baby was born, she had seen the top of his head, dark and wet, in the mirror over the delivery table. "I'm glad!" she had said, or nearly shouted; she had seen her words splash on the white masks around her. Shameless, she had turned back the sheet to admire her body. Stark again, it had retained the look of the labor it had accomplished, like a tractor parked beside a plowed field. She had been so proud that she had not even noticed the sullen silence inside her head. "Seas, seas," the air conditioner crooned, and she leaned forward to listen and heard instead the other: Everyone feels this way, everyone. It's called post partum. . . . The tune rose, sliding over the rest.

Determined to avoid another harangue, she got out of bed and went to the door of her room. She had never opened it before, and she was surprised to find that it was very heavy. She crept out and looked up and down. There was no one in sight, and so she began to walk, following the arrows to the nursery and keeping close to the rank of closed doors.

The broad glass windows of the nursery flashed with light

and she hesitated, wondering who might look out at her from behind the babies. At last she crept forward and looked in. Their boxes stood in a row against the window, each topped with a card of typed facts; she read those before looking at the babies. Two had been born on the same day as her own and she was amazed by that, as though she might share something with those women—a lifelong link, buried in the flesh.

Her own baby lay propped on his side, one mittened fist beating the air. She hated those mittens; when he was brought to nurse, she fingered them tentatively, feeling his fingers inside. Her own mittens had been canvas, tied on at night with stout pink laces; years after she had stopped sucking her thumb, she had seen them hanging from a hook in her closet, like a pair of small chained hands. The baby's mittens were made of flannel, close and soft.

As she watched, he began to cry, his mouth shaping sounds she could not hear. She pressed closer to the glass. A nurse sat on the other side, marking sheets of paper, and for a wild moment, Mina imagined rapping on the glass. Then she noticed that most of the babies were crying while the others lay asleep among them, undisturbed. It seemed the order of things that some should sleep and some should cry while the nurse sat marking her papers. Mina's concern withered and she went back to her room. Closing the door, she was startled by the silence. The air conditioner had stopped its song.

She sat on the edge of her bed, waiting for the voice to start; she expected it to take advantage of the silence. After a while, she began to wonder if the voice and the song had fused so that one could not break out without the other. Leaning back, she heard, for the first time, the dim scurry of traffic outside her window, and then the lunch cart rattling down the hall. All around her, women were sitting up in bed, smiling, pushing back their hair.

When the nurse brought her tray, Mina thanked her profusely and saw a glint of recognition, a submerged smile, in the woman's eyes. Immediately, Mina was ashamed of her misplaced emotion. She ate a leaf of lettuce and two slices of tomato, cold and grained with salt. After a while, the quiet dark-eyed nurse, her favorite, came to take the tray away, and Mina closed her eyes so that she would not have to talk.

As soon as the nurse had gone, the air conditioner picked up its song, quickly, in the middle of a line: "To Ireland." Under it, the other voice marched; hysterical, hysterical, it said. Mina put her fingers in her ears and heard the voice, without the song, plodding in her brain.

She snatched her fingers out. The tune ran over the voice, melting its ferocity. She fixed her attention on the tune; it was essential to find or forge a permanent connection. Ireland. She had been there once on a summer jaunt with her parents; the memory was vague. It had been only one of many carefully planned trips. She did remember that the hotel in Dublin had been something of a fraud, for in spite of its grandeur, it was built over the railroad station. No one had remarked on the constant noise of trains, and Mina had not opened her bedroom curtains to see what lay outside. Finally one night, feeling stifled, she had snatched the curtains back. An iron network of tracks spread below her, leading away as though she were the lode; a long arrangement, precise yet ecstatic where the double lines dissected, curved, and shot off. A small engine was marching there. She had dropped the curtain quickly, feeling the coal soot fret her hand. The next afternoon, in a tea room, she had disagreed with her parents over whether they should order scones or save the calories for dinner and suddenly, passionately, she had declared that she wanted to go home. Her father had ordered the scones as she had wished and her mother had reached across the table to pat her fiery hand. They had seemed to understand why she was so angry, but she had not understood at all. Afterward, she had not been able to mention the scene in order to apologize because the anger stuck in her throat like a splinter of glass.

Obviously, she had not made the right connection with the song: the air conditioner dozed off into silence and she was left alone for the rest of the afternoon. At five, a nurse brought in a large bunch of pink roses, and tears came suddenly into

Mina's eyes. She had not been expecting flowers, and she begged the nurse to take them away: "They'll just make a mess for you, shedding their petals in here." But the nurse told her that good money had been spent on the roses. "And what if your friends come and don't see them!" Mina could not remember the faces of the couple who had sent the roses, and she was ashamed of her vagueness and ingratitude. She got up to wash her face and comb her hair before the baby was brought. She did not want him to find her slovenly.

He took the breast eagerly, without opening his eyes. Mina lay waiting for him to finish. Her nipples were sore, and his strong tug hurt her; she looked down at his avid face and did not relent. He was male, whole and complete, and he would use her for one thing or another for the rest of her life. He was wearing his mittens, and the sight of his blind hand flapping against her arm made her weep. When the nurse came to take him away, Mina asked for a sedative and saw for the second time a gleam of recognition, a shaming understanding in the woman's eyes.

The pill came in a little plastic cup; she licked it up surreptitiously. Then it was time to prepare herself for Stephen. She dreaded visiting hours; then all the doors were open and male voices disrupted the silence of the hall. The men sounded fierce and excitable as they wove their ways between their wives' rooms and the nursery. They came bearing books, flowers, fresh nightgowns, all inessential, yet after they had left, Mina could feel the depression, thick as wax, which sealed the women in their separate rooms.

Stephen burst in exactly at seven, tired, smiling, trailing the hot smells of the city day. He whirled toward her with kisses, the newspaper—white hopes extended. She was ready for him. "Don't you think it's warm in here?"

"A little. I'll turn this thing up." He went toward the air conditioner.

"Yes, please." She waited while he turned the knob; the rush of air increased but the song did not begin. "It's been singing at me all day," she told him gaily.

"What does it sing?" He was used to her whimsy.

"Oh, some foolishness." She was suddenly unwilling to tell him. "Over the seas to Ireland, something like that."

"Did you ask the nurse to give you something?"

"Yes, and she gave me a pill as though she expected it." She was overcome by disparagement and began to cry.

He came and held her solemnly, aware, she thought, of the increased weight of his responsibilities. She wondered if he had felt chained and weighted when he stood beside her in the labor room. "Did you want all this to happen?" she asked.

"Of course!"

"But doesn't it occur to you, even if we didn't want it, even if we changed our minds. . . . I can't remember when I wanted it!"

"Don't you remember, in Vermont?"

"I remember we walked to the top of a hill, through an old orchard. That time in Dublin I wanted to jump out my window and get on a train and go anywhere."

"Alone?"

"I guess that was the point."

"This room is too cut off."

"But it's worse," she said, "when someone is here."

At that the song began, with a shout. She looked at Stephen sharply.

"I brought you the mail—a magazine, and three letters." He turned away, opening his brief case. "Also your beer." When he brought them, she touched his hand.

"You can't hear anything, can you? I know you can't."

"I'm going to turn that damned thing off."

She snatched his arm. "No, don't. It's not the song I mind, it's the voice underneath and that's stopped now."

He smiled at her. "I always thought one voice was enough."

"Oh no! You've got to have two, to count. The talking one keeps saying I'm no good." She made a face like a sad clown and they both laughed.

At nine o'clock, the speaker over Mina's bed announced that visiting hours were over, and Stephen stood up and uncapped a bottle of beer. "For night sadness," he said, and patted her and kissed her and left. Mina drank all the beer as quickly as she could and then lay back in the curve of her pillows. After a while, she began to feel flushed and easy, and she feasted on something Stephen had said: "You make such a pretty mother." He had said it quickly, embarrassed by such obviousness. She wished she had forced him back to repeat and elaborate, to examine her face, her breasts, her thin slack body and tell her that she was all pretty, and well equipped for the task. How surprised he would have been, surprised and, she imagined, a little disappointed; he would have stared at her, seeing the mauve ribbons in her bed jacket and the mauve ribbon in her hair.

The baby was brought at ten o'clock and fastened to her breast by a brisk nurse with red iron hands. Mina's nipples were still sore and the baby drew and drew in a frenzy; he did not seem to get a drop. Mina knew that if she asked, they would give him a bottle, and felt beforehand her guilt and despair. Cruel failures lay on all sides and her successes were as thin as ribbons. The baby would be brought again at two and there was nothing she could do to prevent it except give up, abandon the whole thing. The tight silence of the room pressed against her, molding itself to her body, and she longed for the song of the air conditioner. It purred instead, mechanically tranquil. At last the baby was taken away and she turned out the light and lay, gripped in silence, waiting for two o'clock. It seemed to her that she was being eaten alive.

The nurse who came in at two snapped on the light and dropped the baby like a small bomb on Mina's bed. "Just ten minutes, each side," she warned. "I'll be back for him." This time, the baby's eyes were open and he was not crying. He looked up at Mina calmly, his hands, in the flannel mittens, folded on his chest. She looked at him for a while, aware of the way they were enclosed in the yellow bell of light from the standing lamp. She began to feel, against all reason, that the baby knew her; he looked up at her so confidently, waiting for her to begin. Cautiously, she took his left hand and peeled back the mitten.

She had not seen his hands since the night he was born and for a moment, she was afraid. Then she peeled back the other mitten and held his hands closely, as though to prevent him from doing some harm. Finally, she let them go. His left arm lifted and the hand unfurled slowly, like a leaf. His fingers were thicker than she had expected, with a flake of skin at the corner of each nail to remind her of the way he had grown, week by week, inside her eagerness. Then the air conditioner began to sing. She groaned and caught his hands again, waiting for the voice to start. After a while, she heard it, far off, chanting venomously. Anybody can. Anybody can. Anybody can have a baby. Suddenly the air conditioner's song rose, drowning the voice, which went down with a shriek of vengefulness. "Over the seas!" the air conditioner shouted.

Mina put the baby to her breast and lay back in the pillows. He sucked and sucked and then, for the first time, he began to swallow. She heard his long hard gulps and saw a bubble of milk forming at the corner of his mouth. His bare hand waved as though to set the beat for his delight, and his face, suffused, was the color of a candle flame. She looked at him with amazement. At the same time, she noticed something new, a creamy warmth at the front of her body. Something feels good, she told herself cautiously. She did not want to examine the feeling too closely, and for a while, she thought it was the baby's warm head, pressing against her arm. Finally she realized it was his mouth on her healing nipple.

She was ashamed for a moment, and she heard something whine at the back of her mind. Then the air conditioner's song rose a little, peacefully droning. "Seas, seas." She fell asleep before the baby had finished.

She woke when he was lifted out of her arms. Opening her eyes, she saw the nurse pulling the mitten back over his hand.

A small rage gripped her and she sat up. "I'd like those mittens left off, please."

The nurse glanced at her and smiled. She started to pull on the second mitten, propping the sleeping baby against her hip.

"I want those things left off," Mina said, and this time her light voice rose.

The nurse looked at her.

"He should be able to suck his fingers if he wants to." She was beginning to tremble with rage.

"Don't you know he can't get his hand to his mouth?" the nurse asked kindly. "You want something to help you get back to sleep?"

"No!" Mina shouted. "I want those things off!" A great blush of delight spread over her face.

Sighing, the nurse uncovered the baby's right hand. Mina watched, tigerish, while she freed the other. The sleeping hands curved up like little cups. "Now he'll scratch his pretty face for sure," the nurse said, sighing.

Mina was so surprised that she laughed. It had never occurred to her that there was another reason. "Never mind," she gasped when the nurse looked at her uneasily. Throbbing with laughter, she watched the baby go and remembered that in two more days, she would take him home.

After that she lay awake for a long time, listening to the air conditioner croon its beautiful song. She knew that sooner or later the old voice would break in but she was not afraid: the song and the voice were finally braided together. Among the strands, she thought that she would be able to find her own light voice, but magnified, intense and brilliant as a streak of blood.

FEAR

Turning the knob so slowly it seemed to glide, greased, under her palm, Jean finally opened the baby's door. It was early morning, the pink lambs and blue horses on the curtains just becoming visible; the crib, under its canopy, was still a pit of shadows, and Jean saw the brown bear, the snake, and the cat lined up at the rail, on guard.

She took a step toward the crib and stopped. The baby's smell, made of milk and powder and the soap she used in the washing machine, stood in front of her like a screen. She drew several breaths, trying to believe that since he smelled the same, nothing could be wrong. There had been so much crying the evening before, so much panic and screaming that she thought her observations might have been crazed.

Hearing him stir, she bent down. His eyes were open; he lay on his back, his hands out, and looked up at her as though he had always expected her to be there. "Hello, little duck," she said and reached in to pick him up. His body felt changed to her, limp, yielding; fat as a sack, she thought. Holding him tightly in her arms, she remembered how he had clung to her neck after she had punished him. "I'm sorry, I'm so sorry," she had sobbed, and he had repeated, "Orry."

Then she put him down. As his feet touched the floor, he began to whimper. Turning, he tried to clutch her knees as his legs splayed out. She moved back and he slid to the floor where he sat, whimpering and looking up at her. "You can do it," she whispered cheerily, and picked him up and set him again on his feet. He gave a cry and leaned against her hands. She tried to push him away but he clung, crumpling at the same time at the knees. They're not working, she thought. The legs are still not working. She picked him up and rocked him in his arms.

He stopped crying immediately. "Here's the little kitty," she said, taking the animal out of the crib. As the baby seized the toy, she closed her eyes and buried her mouth in his cheek. It seemed to her that she ought to put him down again, to make sure, but she knew she would not be able to bear his crying. That was what had caused it, in the beginning—his crying. He would start over something so trivial—the cat had been misplaced, in this case—and his crying would wind on and on, endlessly on and on, growing into small shrieks that pierced her head. She had looked frantically for the cat and then, giving up, she had walked the baby up and down, trying to console him. It seemed to her that the crying would never stop. She was trapped inside the sound; the hour of the day and the day of the week drifted away and she was trapped, helplessly, inside the sound of a baby's screams. She had picked him up once more to try to comfort him but instead she had plunged him down onto the floor, plunging him again and again until his cries turned into hysterical screams. Then she had sat beside him on the floor, dazed, gasping for breath, and gone at last to open a window.

Coming back, she had seen him trying to get up.

Now, as she held him in her arms, she knew she had never really hoped, not even in the night when she had felt quite calm, lying against her husband's back. She had never really hoped. As soon as she had seen him trying to get up, she had known that she had hurt him in some terrible way. Her life had shriveled as she watched him, wallowing. She had never loved anyone as she had loved him, since she had felt his first tentative flutter inside her womb. She had been guiltily aware that she loved him more than she could ever love her husband, who was critical at times, and never really hers. But she had never hurt her husband, except glancingly, she had never even scratched the surface of all the offensive strangers she had known, she had hardly ruffled her parents' composure although she had hated them for years, and she had allowed people to disturb and wound her without even frowning. It was the baby she had hurt.

Still carrying him in her arms, she walked into the kitchen. Maria, the housekeeper, was standing at the sink, filling the percolator with water. She glanced at Jean, her eyes glassy and aglow. Jean stopped abruptly. The woman had no way of knowing, had been out of the apartment when it happened. Jean went to the high chair and propped the baby inside its arms; he was still as limp as string. She had to take his hands from her shoulder finger by finger, but this time, he did not cry. He looked at her with his round flat eyes which she had never been able to penetrate; his happy eyes, like buttons. He had always been a happy baby and she had known it was at least partly because she mothered him well, flying to satisfy his demands, giving up her sleep and her freedom too willingly and gladly, as though they had never meant anything at all.

"Will you give him his breakfast, please, Maria? It's so early, I'm going back to bed."

In the hall, she thought, I will wake up John and tell him what happened, and he will tell me what to do.

She opened the bedroom door and the cold breeze from the window lapped against her ankles. Her husband, darkly bundled, lay in the middle of the bed. She stood with the doorknob in her hand, squeezing and turning it. It seemed to her that he must hear the sound and wake up, but he did not stir. She could not see his face, and she wished he would turn over so that she could at least see his eyes, which were generally kind. But he did not move. She had looked at him the evening before, intending to tell him, even imagining a scene with some tears but final comfort; looking at him, she had felt something fearful and cringing rise up inside her, authoritative, too, as though it possessed the final wisdom: do not tell him. No, never tell him. It was as though she had taken a lover, a foul black passion, and must guard with all her strength against the relief of revelation. John had remarked that she was looking pale.

She went out of the bedroom and closed the door. In the kitchen, Maria was talking to the baby. Jean listened to her soft, pattering voice. Borne along on the sound, she went to the front door and opened it. Maria will take care of him, she thought; he will be all right as long as he is with her. She rang the bell for the elevator. The morning paper was lying on the floor, crumpled, a fallen bird; she picked it up and laid it neatly on the bench.

In the elevator, she realized that she was not dressed and looked down at her short housecoat. It would pass; only her slippers gave her away. She took them off and put them in her pocket.

Outside, she felt the gritty pavement under her feet and was frightened. Dog filth and the litter from an overturned garbage pail lay along her way; smoking pyramids of dog filth, torn streamers of paper stained with hamburger blood. She placed each foot heavily, wondering how long it would be before she felt something wet. Crossing the street, she went into the park.

The smoky morning sky lay along the tops of the trees; looking up, she saw the sun burning a hole the size of a penny. The trampled grass, shaggy as an old dog's coat, was lifting a blade at a time. She remembered spreading the plaid wool shawl here for the baby and herding him in from the edges; his white shoes had been as clean when they went as they had been at the start. Walking a little farther, she reached a point where one path led into the interior. The path she always took with the baby stretched along the edge of the street. The other, inside path was rutted from tree roots, and the only bench she could see had lost one of its legs. She had never hesitated before: the choice had been made for her by the sight of the baby's white bonnet, nodding like a peony inside the carriage hood. Now she took the broken path.

It was very early; she had passed one man with a dog, but

otherwise the park was empty. Empty, but edged with sounds and odd half-animate rustlings; she saw a squirrel move down a tree trunk with small crippled feet. She stopped to look back, wondering what the animal expected. His tail was as thin as an old feather. His eyes, however, were shining, and she hurried on, remembering the crib animals at the rail. She thought she heard the squirrel coming after her, on light crippled feet, and turned to shout and wave him away. A small man, muffled in a coat, passed her quickly, his breeze fanning her cheek.

She was so startled she sat down on the broken bench. Above the tops of the trees, the apartment buildings raised their crenelated towers; she looked the other way and saw the little man, hurrying on his small feet, turn the corner and disappear. Awkwardly, she pushed herself up off the bench and followed.

She was out of her territory at once; the plaid shawl had never been spread on these grassy places. She was astonished by the thickness of growth—weeds, mosses, trees; the park, abandoned, had grown up like the back fields of a lost farm. Purple nettles, their heads as big as apples, stood at the edge of the path. The sidewalk, cracked and cracked again by shadows, ran in semicircles down into a little valley where a dry fountain lay half full of leaves.

At the edge of the pool, she stopped. A marble cupid, its flesh green with mold, raised an amputated elbow toward her. Its eyes were marked in the center by straight slits, like a cat's. Jean stood still and waited. Under her feet, the warm sidewalk grew cool and she imagined the green mold starting there and spreading around her like a shallow pool. The sounds of the city, sifted through the leaves, were as remote as summer thunder. She stood until her thighs began to ache, and then she sat down quickly on the lip of the pool.

She knew that she was being watched from the trees, and she sat carefully, her short robe drawn over her knees. Staring into the leaf-filled pool, she showed the back of her neck, bare and white, between her hair and the edge of her collar. As he watched from the shadow, he would catch the glint of white skin. Waiting, she began slowly to freeze, until she knew that soon she would be unable to lift her hand. She moved her head slightly, adjusting it for the last time, and saw that the cupid had a chain of beer-can tops around his neck.

As she waited, a blade of sunlight stretched slowly across the pavement, approaching her feet. After a long time, its point touched her toes, and she saw that she was shod in filth; only her insteps were still white. Revolted, she stood up. She had always hated dirt, any form of dirt, but public dirt collected from the feet of other people was intolerable. As she started purposefully back, she saw the trees, coalesced against her, shrouding the small black hole where the path ran toward the street.

Suddenly, she was afraid. Wishing could make anything happen, might already have set the disaster on its course. She stood prepared to defend herself and examined the ranks of trees. If he was watching, he must see that she was ready, her bare neck hidden now, her fists gripped. She remembered that he had been very small and thought that her assurance alone might quell him. But the wish, the terrible self-fulfilling wish for pain and mutilation still hung in the air above her like a beacon. She knew that he would see it and understand that her defenses were only temporary. Panting, she began to walk slowly toward the entrance.

Sweat ran down the insides of her arms, thick as honey. Her own smell, rank as the weeds', tortured her with its implications; animals, in danger, give off a hot rich stench. Moving carefully, on lead feet, she began to believe that if she could reach the trees, she would be safe. It occurred to her to run, but remotely, dreamily. She kept repeating, doggedly, that she did not want anything to happen, although she knew that her doubt would flash through as her bare neck had flashed, inviting the blow.

Shadows fell over her as heavily; she had reached the trees. She panted. The trees were around her now and she could no longer feel the weight of his eyes. He would be moving closer, in order to keep her in view. Lifting her knees, she began at last to run, jogging clumsily, her breasts jerking. Her body inside the housecoat was as loose and thick as jelly, and she imagined her stomach dropping to her knees. Perhaps if he saw that she had borne a child, he would spare her. At that she began to run more quickly.

Dashing, her flesh quickening, she left the shade of the trees. Below the embankment, a bus stopped and passed on. She could see the faces of the passengers at their windows, and she wanted to call and hold her hands out to them. Running down the slope, she nearly collided with a large woman leading a brace of hounds. The woman muttered and scowled as Jean stared at her. Jean crossed the street, skipping through a stream of cars, and heard their wild cries remotely. Her own building shone in a special patch of sun. She rushed in and flung herself into the open elevator.

As soon as she opened the door of the apartment, she knew that she was too late. The smell of frying bacon still hung in the air, but the baby's dishes were heaped in the sink and his bib was lying like a fallen flag on the floor. She went from room to room, looking carefully, but she knew they had already gone.

Sinking down on the kitchen floor, she fixed her eyes on the linoleum. The history of the apartment, replacing her life, streamed around her, and she wondered if anyone else out of the dozens who had lived there had ever crouched down on the kitchen floor. She remembered picking out the tiles, with much effort and indecision; she remembered her satisfaction as they were laid down. Now the bright blue was melting into the old tiles beneath it and the floor was turning mud-colored again. She had imagined when they had first moved in that she would make a life consciously chosen in every detail, and she had put her hand on her stomach to feel the baby's light kick, sure that this was the first great choice and that the rest would follow. There had been a clear connection between

the daisies she had arranged and her passion for her husband,
between the pablum she had prepared and her love for the
baby that had gradually grown and engulfed all the rest.

I loved him too much, she thought, and that is why they
have taken him away.

Time passed: she heard the big electric clock draw its hand
through several numbers. She did not dare to raise her eyes
from the floor, and the back of her neck and her knees began
to ache. She thought that if they found her like that, kneeling,
they might forgive her. When she heard the front door open,
however, she sprang to her feet, and screamed because of the
cramped pain in her knees.

"Jean?" her husband called.

She ran down the dark hall which lengthened in front of
her, a tunnel with their faces at the end. The baby, wrapped
in a blanket, lay in the crook of Maria's arm; when he saw his
mother's face, he began to cry, reaching out for her with both
hands. Still too far away to touch him, she held out her arms,
and her husband took the child and placed him in her hands.
She did not dare to move him closer; she held him out at the
ends of her arms, which trembled under his weight.

John pressed the baby against her chest, and she saw Maria's
face, dark, without any smile. She turned to look at her husband. His hands, at her back and the baby's back, held them
clamped together, but he was looking away. "He's all right,
isn't he?" she asked softly.

"It was just a bruise, wasn't it?" Neither of them answered.
"Then what was it?" she asked, her voice rising.

"The doctor couldn't find anything wrong," John said finally. "He examined him, but he couldn't find anything
wrong."

"But he couldn't walk! This morning—" She stopped herself.

Maria lifted the baby out of her arms and set him on the
floor. He stumbled forward, his hands stretched toward the
gleaming doorknob.

Jean sobbed.

"It's all right now," John said, touching her arm.

"But what happened?"

John looked away. The gap of their silent understanding widened between them; Jean knew they would never speak of what she had done.

The baby had reached the doorknob and was patting it with his hand.

PLEASE NO EATING NO DRINKING

It was terrible to look back, it was sometimes even more terrible to look forward, but the present, the everyday, was quite pleasing; Louise thought of that as soon as she woke and saw her white curtains. She darted out of bed, her feet flying for her slippers, which lay where she could step into them without looking. Then, winged by her nightgown, she went into the bathroom, which was sweet with the smells of the perfume and powder she had worn the day before. The roar of water running into the tub filled her head and she did not think again until she was naked.

Then, inadvertently, she looked down. Her glance caught on the sharp hook of her hip, straining against flat flesh. Next she saw her legs, knobbed with knees like bedposts, and her really old feet, the toes hunched and curled, the heels silver with shaved callouses. Age had happened to her at a certain moment in her life, like an explosion; the reverberations made her reel, then passed into silence, and she was once again a young girl stepping into her tub.

The trouble was, she thought, that marriage had taken up so much of her life. Twenty years at hard labor could not have aged her so drastically. You are killing me! she had cried with her pallor, her extinguished eyes; but all the time she had felt a secret wild glee. The idea of the divorce had come in the end from him. It had taken her some time to learn to sleep and eat without him, but after that, the luxury of living alone was a delight to her. Even the presence of her daughter did not dilute the pleasure she took in eating at any hour or dozing or simply sitting, quiet as a bunch of flowers in an empty room.

After her bath, she put on the clothes she had laid out the night before. Her dress slid over her like a blessing. There was nothing sharp or bulging to catch the sliding silk; she felt it pass her hips and thighs smoothly. It had taken her most of her life to begin to enjoy herself, the self defined by long bones and narrow flesh, and now she looked with admiration at the person she had made, a city woman, a worker, a lovely female, delicately outlined in the full-length mirror. Then she went to make herself a cup of coffee.

While she was drinking it, she heard a door close and called, "Katy, is that you?" It would have been a pleasant surprise to find her daughter up in time to share her breakfast. There was no reply, and she knew that Katy, partly wakened, had only stumbled up to shut her door. She always left it open a crack at night—an old habit, which she should have outgrown. Louise had spoken to her about it, once or twice. As a result, Katy closed her door as soon as she woke in the morning, but since she never woke as early as her mother, it did no good. Louise smiled as she thought of the big warm girl in her flannel pajamas. In another year, when she went away to college, their companionship would have to end. But for the time being, it was very nice to have Katy at home, filling the apartment with her special silence.

Having finished her coffee, Louise went back to her room to make the bed. She liked to leave the room complete and ready so that when she came home, she would find it waiting for her, the silk bedspread still warm from the sun. She often thought fondly of her bedroom while she was at work; it depended on her to begin its life. She flicked the sheets out flat and dangled each of the four pillows by its corners. The cases were covered with pink roses. It was all so fresh, and fine; but she remembered when that same bed had been a catastrophe every morning, a scene of destruction to be covered hastily with a cotton spread. There was something obscene about two people living together which had nothing to do with sex. They made such a clutter, of possessions, feelings, touches. She patted the silk quilt down. There. That would do for now. Smiling, she picked up her purse and gloves.

At the door, she called "Good-by!" and imagined the word lighting on Katy's sleeping face. She would wake to the alarm at eight-thirty and go into the kitchen to drink the rest of the coffee. Their days were interleaved, although they seldom saw each other. Sometimes in the early evening Katy would come and sit on the side of the bed while Louise was dressing to go out. (Louise had given up asking her not to rumple the spread since with Katy's weight, it was impossible to sit down without displacing or rumpling something.) They would talk then, or at least Louise would talk, telling about her day. Katy, listening, her chin propped on her fist, would rock back and forth and Louise, in spite of herself, would imagine the imprint of those large white buttocks on the silk, on the blanket, and finally on the sheets.

At the corner, Louise bought a newspaper and clutched it under her arm as she ran for the bus. Fortunately, there was an empty seat between two empty seats where she could sit at her ease, free of strange elbows and thighs. She opened her newspaper and spread it in front of her face.

On the front page, she read that a boy had set himself on fire in front of the United Nations. When they had put him out, he had apologized for the trouble he was causing; he had not seemed to know why he had done it. Looking up, Louise saw the pale green of the park trees.

It was spring, and spring did terrible things to people; she turned to the second page. It did no good to sympathize too much, to bleed over every disaster. The city was full of horrors—she had always known that. On one of the first nights after Charles had left, she had heard someone screaming in the street. Running to the window, she had looked out, but the street below was empty; across, in the dark shrubbery, the screams had ceased abruptly. She had looked in the newspaper the next day, but there had been no explanation. For a woman, living alone in the city meant a certain hardening. If she had seen the boy burning, she would have screamed for help, but at the same time, she would have wondered what he thought he was accomplishing.

One of her men friends—she liked to call them that, for the double irony of it—had told her that all this adolescent business, the marching, the long hair, was in some strange way a branch of the American dream. "We have lost our material hardships," he had explained, leaning toward her, his bald pate shining like the full moon, "and so we have lost the passion which made us endure and all that lost passion must live on, somehow, in them." He had sounded like a book reviewer then, which was what he was, and she had told him that she was not enclosed in any such collective loss. "I'm managing," she had said. "I'm sometimes nearly happy, and look! I've lost everything."

"You only lost what you didn't want," he had said, which had made her a little angry.

Still it was a comfort to know the Katy, in spite of her weight and untidiness, was basically settled and happy: at the top of her class in school, assured of a place in a good college —her life spread out in peaceful perspectives. At college she would doubtless find a beau and go on a diet. Louise did not take much credit for her daughter's successes; Katy had been born quiet and purposeful, from the beginning quite undemanding. Still it was a relief and a joy to set back and watch the girl moving steadily along.

At Seventy-ninth Street she disembarked with her brief case and swung down the sidewalk to the private library. Inside, the tall cool hall smelled faintly of spring: there was a pot of purple hyacinths on the librarians' table. Louise thought of bringing them some flowers herself, one day; they were grim old women, lined up like judges behind their high desk. "Good morning!" she called and they answered in unison. She swung up the stairs, and passed into the reading room.

At that hour in the morning, it was always empty. She took her usual seat beside the window and spread her papers on

the desk. It was a seat which later in the day was often occupied by a man; the light there was too harsh for most women.
Having laid out her eraser and two pencils, she was ready to
begin. She was finishing the translation of a book of Russian
poetry, for which she would be paid well, although not well
enough. It amused her that the language which she had labored on so at college, and which everyone had assured her
was, for a pretty girl, a complete waste of time, should have
come in the end to have such practical value. For honor's
sake, she had insisted on a meager alimony, far less, in fact,
than Charles had wanted to give her, and so the money she
made on her brisk translations meant the difference between
buying a new dress once a month and once a year. It also
meant that she could rent a car on the weekend and have her
hair done every Thursday. She enjoyed supplying herself with
these amiable luxuries, which she could not have accepted
from Charles, now that she was no longer fulfilling her part
of the bargain. She felt differently about Katy's support money,
which was more than adequate. Katy, poor child, used very
little of it for herself, having no interest in the pleasures of
the flesh.

She was well into her work, the words humming and throbbing around her, her neat script pinning each one down, when
she noticed that two people had come into the reading room.
One of them slid into the low armchair next to her desk. She
could not understand why he had chosen that chair when every
other seat in the room was empty and, surreptitiously, she
pulled her skirt down. Then she noticed that he was tilting
his head to catch the sunlight on his face. He was very thin
and bloodless, with a cultivated air of suffering; she saw his
white ankles flash as he crossed his legs. It was spring vacation,
she remembered—Katy's first day—and no doubt this young
man had come into the library to make up overdue work. Then
she noticed that he had a magazine in his lap, and went back
to her papers. She wished he had not sat so close; she could
even hear him breathing.

The other person was still lurking on the far side of the

room. Sun-blinded, she did not see him clearly until he came to the magazine table. He was a middle-aged man, portly and somewhat disheveled; his overcoat hung open like a pair of heavy doors. His cuff links flashed, too large and too bright, as he turned over the current issues. Still, he had a certain air; his hair, which was either white or very blond, stood up like a wing. She watched him move around the table, issue by issue, until he was quite close; then, to her surprise, he turned toward her, raising his hand in a little salute.

She stared. Then, as he approached, she shrank back. At the edge of her desk, he leaned over the boy's chair.

The boy looked up and smiled. The light fell on his teeth and Louise saw something liquid and lively, nestled inside his gums—his tongue, of course. They knew each other, then. She turned back to her work. A minute later, the sharp crackle of paper forced her to look up: the older man was opening a chocolate bar. It was a large chocolate bar and he was peeling it slowly, bit by bit. The silver paper caught the light and flashed dim patches onto their rapt faces. All at once Louise felt that she had reached her limit. She pushed back her chair.

"Don't you see the sign?" she asked them.

They looked at her, amazed, as though they had not noticed her before. Their wide eyes reminded her of children's, or cows'.

"The sign!" she repeated, exasperated, and she picked up the cardboard square on her desk. "It says Please no eating no drinking."

"I'm so sorry," the older man said. "I didn't know we were disturbing you."

"You're not disturbing me. But there is a rule."

"I'm so sorry," he repeated humbly. As though to appease her, he moved off slowly and sat down on a couch, his hands folded around the chocolate.

She tried to work, after that; she bent her head almost down onto the paper, but it was no use. The room seemed stifling and she wanted to take off her beads and open the tight collar of her dress. Every time the boy turned a page, she heard it;

every time the older man sighed or cleared his throat, she lost her place in the text. Finally she stood up abruptly and started to gather her papers. They both glanced at her and she wanted to tell them—but quietly, with understanding—"This is not the time, or the place." Instead, she snatched her coat and strode out.

On the bus going home, she grew calm. It would be nice to have lunch with Katy for a change, as a celebration of spring and her first day of vacation. There were two ripe tomatoes in the refrigerator, half a can of tuna fish, and some mayonnaise Louise had made herself. She imagined the two of them, in strange domesticity, combining the ingredients for their lunch.

Going into the apartment, she called out, "I'm home early, Katy!" and laid her brief case on the bench. She waited, expecting the girl to come out of her room. The apartment was very quiet, and Louise realized that she did not know its look in the middle of the day. There was dust on all the table tops, a fine soft growth like moss. Going to the kitchen, she saw her coffee cup alone on the edge of the sink. So Katy was asleep. In spite of herself, she felt a little disappointed: the first day of vacation deserved something better, surely, than a long morning in bed. Without knocking, she went into Katy's room. The shade was drawn and in the grainy dark, she saw the girl's bed, tumbled and empty. After all, then, she had made some arrangement for herself. Louise smiled as she lifted the shade, letting sunlight into the disorderly room. Stepping over shoes and underwear, she went toward her own door.

Her blue silk spread was lying in a heap on the floor. Stepping across it quickly, she saw her flowered sheets, pulled apart and trailing; the pillows were piled up like a wall. In their shade, Katy was lying curled, one plump arm dangling toward the floor.

"What are you doing in my bed?" Louise asked.

Katy sighed and Louise bit her lip to keep from shouting. She had left the bed fresh and finished and now she would have to make it all over again. "Get up, Katy," she said.

She leaned down and touched Katy's hand. It was a large, soft hand, like a mound of dough, as unformed now as it had been when she was ten. "Rise and shine, lazybones," Louise said, mastering her irritation. "I came home early to have lunch with you."

The girl still did not move and Louise suddenly imagined having to heave her great body out of the bed. "What's the matter with you?" she asked crisply. "Don't you hear what I'm saying?"

Katy turned her head and looked at her mother. "I like it in your bed," she said. "It smells like you."

"Out of there at once, young lady," Louise said, taking hold of the edge of the sheet.

Katy lifted her arm and the sheet, slightly pulled, slipped off her. Louise had not seen her naked for several months and her eyes raced over the rounded heap of her stomach and her big low breasts, the nipples gaping like mouths. "What happened to your nightgown?" she asked, a little dazed.

Katy reached above her head and stretched. As she arched her back the sharp black triangle of her pubic hair stood up. Louise dropped the sheet. She knew immediately, as she had at the library, that she had reached her limit. "This is all very amusing, but I want you out of there and dressed in five minutes flat."

"I can't get up, Mama."

"Why in the world not?"

"I just can't get up. Not today, anyhow," Katy added, thickly.

Louise stared at her. "Have you been drinking?"

"Just water," Katy said, waving at the table beside the bed. A pill bottle lay on its side near the empty water glass.

Louise snatched the bottle. It was about half empty, and she tried to remember how many she had already used, herself. "How many did you take?"

"A few. Not many. Just enough to sleep all day. Don't worry, I know how many. I've done it before." Yawning, Katy turned over and buried her face in the pillow.

Louise looked up her doctor's number and dialed rapidly. When the nurse answered, Louise said, "Oh Miss Ewing? Is the doctor in?" But as she was making the connection, Louise began to cry, and when the doctor picked up the telephone, he did not immediately understand who it was who was calling.

CONVERSATIONS

John Heller did not like parties, on principle; he was against the waste of hope and time, although he usually enjoyed himself. Food and wine were important to him, and the people he knew could be counted on to provide the best of both, as well as a rather intense form of general conversation. He liked to remember that somebody's aunt, up from the South, had accused him of being a parlor liberal; and he had been mistaken once, during a whole dinner, for the distinguished poet who was so boring no one could believe he was the guest of honor. John Heller was not distinguished, but he was charming and quiet and sane; he looked like an editor of a small but profitable publishing house and women often talked to him about books. He liked the simple contacts with women which dinner parties provided: a shared sofa, a table too crowded for comfort, even the look of two coffee cups set together on the edge of a tray. He had been married a long time, his children were grown, and his wife had retreated into the secret business of middle age. So he nourished himself on the warm impersonal closeness of strange women at small parties, and rejoiced in details he would never have noticed in the grip of intimacy: how one matched her eye shadow to her earrings and another, more distrait, let her long locks dangle down her cheeks.

When he first saw Helen Phelps, sitting in a red velvet chair beside a newly lit fire, John thought she was the prettiest girl he had ever seen. Then he had to correct the exaggeration: her face was constantly disrupted by small grins and frowns. When she grinned—and it was not a smile; there was too much appetite in it for that—her lips drew far back, revealing bright pink gums and small, overlapping teeth. As for the frowns, they graphed her face with lines which were fine and slightly sooty, like the hairlines in an old porcelain plate. She was inexpertly made up, with a great daub of white under each eye, and her blond hair hung in a tassel down her back. Yet she was smooth and shiny in the midst of her disorder, and he imagined that she had a tart fresh smell and a body that was both fleshy and firm. She was very funny, too, although he knew from her startled expression that her remarks were not always planned to amuse. He listened to her and looked at her during the interminable dinner and afterward went to sit beside her on the sofa. They talked a while; she nodded often and enthusiastically without hearing much of what he said. Later, her husband came to say that it was time to leave and Helen stood up, still talking and smiling, held one hand out to John, and extended the other toward the sleeve of her coat. Her husband lifted out the tassel of hair and they went to the elevator together.

"I liked that blond girl, the Phelps girl," John's wife said when they were going home together.

"Is that her name?"

"She used to be Helen Meyer before she married young Franklin. That's four or five years ago now."

"I liked her too," John said.

"Yes, she's a nice little creature." Maria was looking out the cab window; a street light caught the sharp shine of her diamond earring. Beyond it, her profile was dim and soft, scarcely more than shadow.

John waited for a week and then he looked up Franklin Phelps in the telephone book and called, quite early on a Tuesday morning. Helen answered on the third ring with a kitchen clatter behind her. A child was singing piercingly, "Old Macdonald had a farm!"

"Hello? Stop it, Frank," she said. There was an interval while she reconstructed John's identity, and then she said, "Oh, yes!" The child began to sing again. "Eeyi Eeyi oh."

"You sound busy," John said.

"Just the usual morning chaos. It takes me until noon to get myself organized."

"I know what you mean. Mine are all away at school now, so there's a gap in the morning."

"How sad," she said, as though she meant it.

"I was wondering if you would like to have lunch with me one day."

She was not quick enough to answer before a giant pause had loomed. "I'd love to," she said finally.

"Good. What days are best for you?"

"Well, just about any day. I mean most days are equally bad."

"What about next Thursday?" The child had begun to rap on the table and John was eager to end the conversation.

"I guess that'll be all right," she said, then added with fresh spirit, "That will be lovely!"

John told her where to meet him and said good-by. He heard the clatter in the kitchen for a moment before she hung up.

He had never lived in chaos, in fact; his children had been brought up according to the old rules and there had always been plenty of help. He wondered if Helen kept her smiles and frowns for evening or lavished them indiscriminately on her young. Her disorder now had a functional explanation: "Get out! Mommy's trying to fix her face!" The white daubs under her eyes must have represented the singing child's irrepressible invasion. These explanations did not detract from her charm; she still seemed lively and fragmented to him, like a splintered drop of mercury. He was glad that he had told her to meet him at his club, which was usually deserted at lunchtime.

Knowing that she had never been there before, had perhaps never been out to lunch at all except for cottage cheese at a girl friend's, he was careful to arrive early and to notify Sid, the doorman, that he was expecting a guest. Then when she swept in in her mink . . . He smiled to think of Sid's faceless discretion, encountering Helen herself.

He was in the smoking room reading the second section when Sid came to announce that she had arrived. She was exactly five minutes late, and John imagined the elaborate planning which had resulted in such perfect timing. As he went downstairs, he saw her standing alone in the center of the hall. She was wearing a green suit, closely buttoned, and from the way she held her gloves, limply, in one hand, he knew she had never worn them before. Ordinarily, she would sport red mittens. She looked distressed when she found him beside her, and he realized that she was not quite sure who he was. He took her hand, which was very cold. "How nice of you to be so prompt!"

"I was afraid I was going to get here before you," she said. "I didn't know what I would do!"

"They allow ladies to wait in there." He waved toward a chintz-hung alcove.

"But what if I'm not a lady?" she said with an agonized smile.

"You're every inch a one," he said with true fine blarney and took her thin arm to guide her to the elevator.

She asked for sherry before lunch and then sat turning her glass as though she could not bring herself to drink it. "Liquid gold," she said, raising the glass for a ray of sun to strike through.

"But not too precious to drink." He had already finished his first Bloody Mary.

"I get so woozy," she explained, "especially in the middle of the day. Frank and I used to have a drink before lunch on Saturdays but we had to give it up; it conked me out for the whole afternoon."

"And then who would take the children to the park?"

"Frank's pretty good at that. We have an arrangement. On Saturdays, he takes them in the afternoon. . . ." She stopped. "This can't be very interesting for you."

"Yes, it is."

"Don't you want to talk about books or the theater?"

"I get that all the time. What I miss are the plain things."

"Well, I guess once your children are grown . . ." She did not finish the sentence and he did not contradict her. Her knuckles, he noticed, were red as roses, although her short square fingernails had been lacquered a dull pink.

"How old are yours now?" she asked him.

He had drifted far off, looking at her overworked hands, and it took him a while to gather the details she wanted. Then, as he told her about his girls, he began to grow warm, remembering the look and feel of those lost children. He did not like them so much now that there was no excuse to touch them. They wanted to argue with him, to govern him with their energy, and he put up with their belligerence because it did not really matter. He had loved them when they were little, two plump blond girls who had clustered around him so tightly that sometimes he could hardly breathe. Their tears had kept him at home in the evening when Maria longed to go out, their desolate cries had waked him in the middle of the night, and in the morning, before the alarm, he had thrust himself out of bed to go and lift them up, feasting on the stale warm smell of their flannel pajamas, delighting even in the richly soaked diapers which seemed to him proof of life. In everything except the bearing of them, he had been essential.

He began to sink back into a familiar lethargy as he talked about them and, afraid that Helen would notice, he jerked up from the deep chair and waved her toward the dining room. She went ahead of him, peering and wrinkling her nose. The club rooms were dim as caves in the middle of the day, and they passed great throngs of empty leather chairs. In the dining room, he had reserved a table by the window, and there the sun burst in on them at last, showing the papery dryness of her fair skin and the lines around her neck. As a girl, he thought, she would have been too pretty, satiating, but through use and wear she had become delicate and fine. She worried over the menu. "Shall I have the fish?" she asked, but he told her to order the steak. Pleased to have the decision made, she sat back with a sigh. When the platter was passed to her, she stabbed raptly at the tenderloin, then kept the serving fork and began to eat with it. He watched her stop and look at the enormous tines and almost laughed with pleasure when, quite simply, she speared another small piece of meat. Her mouth stretched to receive the fork but her expression remained pleased and calm. He forgot to eat, watching her.

"Aren't you hungry?" she asked.

"I had a late breakfast."

The red meat made her flushed and confident and she looked at him for the first time with a bold sparkle. "What do you do all day?"

"I manage my affairs."

"Does that mean I shouldn't have asked?"

"Not at all. I worked for a while on Wall Street, but it didn't interest me. I have enough money to get along, and that's what I do."

"Don't you get bored?"

"Not unless I wake up very early in the morning. What did you think I did?"

She looked at him appraisingly, the enormous fork in midair. "Oh, I thought you worked on one of the little magazines."

"I've always had a literary flavor, I don't know why. Actually books don't interest me much, or magazines, either. I like to eat and drink and sit in attractive rooms and have friends to gossip with and children to pat."

"That's not asking much."

"Yes, it is," he said.

"You mean you haven't had that?"

"I suppose I did for a time. Then things got in the way: other people's expectations. They weren't mine, but I started to feel that they ought to be."

"You mean having a job, and so forth?"

"Especially the so forth. I don't enjoy that, you see."

She was clearly baffled. "Yet you have two children."

"You don't understand. It's just the trappings I don't care for."

"Oh." Afraid to ask any more questions, she picked the lemon

slice out of her tea and slowly sucked the juice. Delicately, she
spat the seeds into her cupped hand. Then, her plate bare, her
water glass three-quarters empty, her tea gone, and her napkin
carefully refolded, she sat back. "I can't tell you how nice
this is. Generally I have a peanut-butter sandwich with the
kids."

"And don't you ever get bored?"

"Oh, no." She shrugged deprecatingly. "I like them, I really
do. They're really nice, most of the time. Of course, sometimes
I get tired and feel as though it's going to go on forever. But
then I remind myself that when I'm forty, they'll both be in
college. No, I really like it a lot," she added thoughtfully.

"Girls or boys?"

"One of each. Two and five. The baby is a girl."

"What color hair?"

"More or less like mine—mousy. They both have Frank's
brown eyes. Oh, and Gail has a little red in her hair."

"Don't let them grow up too fast," he said.

"You sound just like my mother." Catching herself, she
glanced at him sharply.

He reached across and took her hand, which was curved
around her glass. Carefully, he undid it from the glass and
raised her palm to his mouth. She gave a little shudder. Then
she snatched her hand back and wiped it across her lap.

"I'm sorry," she said quickly.

"I like you," he said. "You have some of the taste of the
earth about you, and that's what I miss."

"With that beautiful wife?"

"That's not exactly what I mean."

"Well, please don't kiss my hand again, if it was a kiss," she
said with an agitated laugh.

"I won't do anything that bothers you. You can depend on
that." He pushed back his chair and went to help her up. At
the dining-room door, he took her elbow and felt the long
quiver which ran down her arm. He had not expected her to be
so highly tuned. "Will you have lunch with me again?" he
asked.

"Why yes, I'd love to." She said it gaily, glancing up at him, aware of the independent response of her arm.

"And someday let me come and see your children."

It would have been too much to ask if he had not been holding her elbow. She could only reply meekly, "Well, we'll have to see about that. They're not very well behaved."

"I never cared much about manners."

In the front hall, Sid brought her brown tweed coat and slipped it over her shoulders. She glanced back at him with vague apprehension. John led her through the tall doors out onto the street. The early winter afternoon shattered against their faces in firy points of freshness and cold. "I guess I'll take the uptown bus," she said.

He walked with her to the bus stop, his hand still under her arm. She had separated herself now from the place where he was touching her, and she was chattering quickly and gaily. He stood with her until the bus came and watched her step up through the doors. When the bus started, she lurched and caught a strap, her face pale and luminous as she stared back at him. He was suddenly apprehensive. She was so frail and young and her needs lay so close to the surface. Then he remembered that he had made himself quite clear, as clear, at least, as he could be without giving it all a name. She would understand, when she thought back over the lunch, that he did not intend to upset her, that he only wanted a small taste of her life. He turned around to walk back to the club. Already the bright afternoon was shading into purple.

He waited ten days before telephoning her again. She agreed with alacrity to meet him the following Monday, and he knew that she had been giving him some thought. "Let's go to the same place," she said. "I liked it so much!" He thought that she was building a myth around him, and imagined with some pleasure the way he would be transformed: brooding rather than bland, more anguished than exhausted. It occurred to him that he had not been depressed for days.

She was fifteen minutes late arriving, and when he went downstairs at last, he found her waiting in the hall, wearing a large black mink. "I didn't like to check it," she explained, holding out her rough hand. Wrapped in fur, she looked astonishingly gray and childlike, yet she held out her hand with authority. This time, she ordered a Bloody Mary and drank it in several gulps, raising her face like a pigeon drinking rain. Then she looked at him with a smile which showed her spring-pink gums. She had a great deal to tell him, she said, but when she began, it was only the facts which he already knew: her husband's name and age, her children's names and ages, all tossed out with gloss and abandon like flowers at his feet. "When I think how tied down I've always been!" she cried. "I was only eighteen when I married, you know."

"That sounds like a song," he said a little sourly.

Halfway through lunch, she began to fade. The radiance which had flooded her face died out and she looked sallow and tired. "Maybe it was a mistake to come here again," she said.

"I don't know why."

She hesitated. "Well, you seem less pleased."

"I'm delighted to see you."

She leaned toward him suddenly, across the littered table. "But you haven't kissed my hand," she said with a jerking laugh, and she held it out to him as though it was a plate.

He printed his mouth on it in the usual way.

"Thank you," she said. "Now you see why I can't call myself a lady." Her streaked eyes filled with tears.

"Please," he said. "I didn't mean to upset you." He stood up hastily, afraid that she might put her face down on the tablecloth.

She stood up, staggering slightly. He put his arm around her waist and led her gingerly to the elevator. He had an impulse to thrust her in and turn away, but he stayed; her warmth was streaming through the thick fur coat. "You must be burning up," he said.

"It's my mother's, really." The words were formed slowly and carefully, against a tide of tears.

"Your mother again," he said, attempting a laugh, but she had forgotten the connection.

Outside the door, she pulled away, fierce with disappointment. "I'm going to take a taxi home."

"You'll be able to dismiss the sitter early. I hope there's no minimum involved."

"Please," she said, "why did you ask me out? Why did you want to get me started?"

"I didn't know you were so startable. I'm sorry," he said, shaking his head. "Everything I say sounds vicious, and I like you so terribly much."

"Then we'll have lunch together again?"

"Certainly. I'll give you a call." He waved down a cab, opened the door, and placed her inside carefully, as though he were returning a fledgling to its nest. Through the back window, he saw her gray eyes darting, and wondered why she had begun so quickly to falter and slide.

He had been moved himself, more than he had realized. The next morning, he woke at his old time, six o'clock, and listened for the children's voices. Then he lay in the darkness a little longer. He believed that he would die at six o'clock one morning with the sheet turned down neatly under his chin. Across the room, his wife lay along the edge of her bed, her hand trailing the floor. She had moaned and tossed in the night, but now she lay quite still. Once she had asked a great deal of him, making scenes, falling on her knees, but he had held out against her clamor and hated her muddy tears. Now he hated her immobility. He got out of bed and went over and looked at her. After a little, he sat down on the edge of her bed. She did not stir; a blade of soft gray hair waved across her forehead like a tentacle. He reached down and picked up her hand and laid it on the bed. Then he got up and went to the kitchen, padding softly down the dark hall.

He boiled an egg and heated the coffee left from the night before and ate at the brilliant formica counter. Outside, the ledges of the courtyard windows were trimmed with stiff new snow. He went back to dress in the half-dark bedroom, and his wife stirred and turned on her side, toward the wall. Taking his gloves, he went out to the hall to get his galoshes, overcoat, and umbrella. The elevator man told him that it was twenty-eight degrees outside, and he buttoned his overcoat up to his chin. Under the canopy, he stopped to open his umbrella; the snow was still falling in even small flakes. He started out, walking in a narrow path between two banks of snow.

At the corner, someone touched his arm. The face was familiar, although altered by a gray knit helmet. "I'll walk you wherever you're going," the man said.

John was as quick as he had ever been.

"You're Franklin Phelps."

"Yes. I'm going downtown. Is that your way?"

"I'm going to Sixty-fifth Street."

"Sixty-fifth and where?"

"Madison."

"That's fine for me."

It was impossible to walk side by side on the narrow cleared path. Frank took to the snow after a few steps. "I didn't want to telephone," he said. "She's in a state this morning. My boy is at school until noon but she has the girl at home."

"And no help."

"That's it. We tried to get a girl up from Jamaica but they're tightening up on that kind of thing. If she got more rest, it might make a difference."

"I'm sure it would."

"She had a hard time as a child. Parents divorced, the works. She was sent away to school when she was eight. I got her to go to a doctor after our little girl was born, but it didn't seem to help. Too much early damage. I try to make up for it, but you can only do so much. Mornings, evenings, and weekends. There's only so much time, so much energy."

John was beginning to hate him.

"It's not that she's psychotic or anything like that. Just tired and sad most of the time. You wouldn't believe it from seeing her dressed up, all smiles and jokes."

"I certainly didn't believe it."

"Now you see she'll be down for weeks. She's always been

this way, trying to make friends out of people who hardly know she exists. She had a bad time last winter over the girl who came in to clean. She thought she quit because she didn't care."

"I'm sorry," John said.

Frank continued to hop along beside him in the snow. "I know this is asking a great deal, but could you take her out to lunch once or twice more? It would get her through the winter. She always has a hard time once the weather turns cold."

"I'm sorry." John held out his hand. "I don't see how I can help you."

Frank tapped his hand away. "You could take her anywhere, to Schrafft's, it wouldn't matter, if you don't want to be seen with her at your club. There are the children to think of, you see."

"Good-by." He stepped off the curb and flagged down a passing cab.

Frank grabbed his arm. "At least give me something to tell her, an excuse or something."

"I don't have any excuse," John said. He reached for the handle and opened the door. The floor of the cab was several inches deep in water from melted snow, and he climbed in with caution and rested his feet on the hump.

Franklin's face hung outside the taxi window like a long gray moon. "But I have to tell her something," he said.

"Tell her I don't exist," John said, as the taxi pulled out into the traffic.

RACHEL'S ISLAND

Since the beginning of hot weather, Jake had been saving the snapshot which his wife's sister had enclosed in her first letter from Nantucket. The snapshot was over-exposed, and the summer house it showed seemed to rise through mists, fragilely anchored to the dunes by bayberry and scrub pine. To Jake, it seemed a clapboard castle, straining against the wind. He kept the snapshot under the socks in his bureau drawer, an unplayed card in the long hand of the summer.

Finally in August he wrote her that he was coming. By then, he was worn as thin as an old dime. The heat had done it, and the tedium of finishing his second novel in the midst of summer parties, summer outings, all set to his wife's fretful drone. Seal-like, she surfaced now and then in the middle of his life, streaming complaints. My life is nothing, she would say; give me a child or I will die. I will leave my job, I will take a lover, I will claim the same rights as you. Usually she sank down again almost at once; Jake had potent ways of reassuring her. That August, she stayed above water a long time.

Yet when he told her that he was going to Nantucket, she did not protest. Their old rules still held and she told him with bitter objectivity, "Go, it'll do you good." He had not really decided to go, and he was irritated with Ann for reacting so predictably. He left the next morning on the bus for Woods Hole.

During the trip, his preoccupations paid out behind him,

growing more tenuous as the city fell away. He sat by a window and watched the landscape flatten and bleach as they approached the ocean. After a while, the old man in the seat across the aisle leaned over and began to talk. He said that he had wanted to go to California since he was eight years old, and now he knew he would never go. Jake had nothing comparable to offer, and on an impulse, he told the old man he was in love. "With someone who don't love you," the old man shrewdly remarked, and after that, Jake sat peacefully under a gentle rain of advice.

The old man did not get off the bus at Woods Hole, and Jake had to face the ferry trip alone. It was beginning to rain, a sharp penetrating drizzle, and Jake regretted the trouble he was taking. It seemed to him suddenly that his sister-in-law was not likely to appreciate his visit, and he felt rejected beforehand, forlorn. The island, as the ferry approached it, looked bleak and unwelcoming. Jake had some difficulty finding a taxi, but at last the arrangement was made and he was driven, in the gathering dusk, down an empty highway. It was a desolate place, in the failing light. Scrub growth covered the sand like a thick tight hide and the wind poured across from the ocean to the bay without a tree or a hill to stop it.

At last they turned onto a sand track and approached the house. It was much smaller than Jake had expected, with a shabby, summer-cottage air; the gray paint was peeling and the windows rattled in the evening wind. His sister-in-law came out onto the porch with the baby at her hip. She looked like a farm woman, Jake thought, with her coarse dark hair and her skirt wind-whipped around her. "Here you are," she said.

There was sand in the front hall and, on the stair landing, a wine bottle stuck full of reeds. Genteel poverty, Jake thought, prodding the thin mattress in his room. Except for the yellow jug on the table, it could have been the room where he had grown up: bald, bare, uncomplained-of, a room where nothing could happen. He took his typewriter out of the case and placed it on the table. Then he went downstairs. His sister-in-law had laid out a plate of cold chicken and a bottle of pickles;

she walked up and down while he ate, jiggling the fretful baby. "He's colicky," she said.

During the night, Jake was wakened by a burst of rain, shattering on the tree outside his window. A little later, the baby started to cry. The storm had had a certain natural grandeur, but the child's wail was another thing altogether, galling as a dripping tap. Jake tossed irritably. After a long time, he heard his sister-in-law go in, but the crying continued, winded and mechanical. At last she began to carry the baby up and down. The floor boards creaked as she placed her feet, solidly, calmly, with only a pretense of stealth, as though, Jake thought, she were stalking a sure prey. His sleep was her prey; she could not fail to know that. She could keep him awake until morning by tramping up and down. He had hardly noticed her before, she seemed so plain and neutral, but now when he sat up to pound on the wall, his fist fell back as though she had pressed her face, moon-smooth, unperturbable, through that section of matchboard. It was not her house, it was rented with her husband's money, she had no power to incorporate its elements. Thin light patched the windows, scoured the room of shadows, and still she walked. Below the bluff, the sea gasped and subsided and gulls clanged up and down the shore. At six, Jake went to sleep, his head under her feet.

Four hours later, he stumbled downstairs. The house was empty, the doors set open to the morning sun. Rachel's breakfast dishes, in the drainer, were already dry, and the baby's bib was pasted to the back of a chair. Jake made himself some instant coffee; it was very bitter, and he could not find the bread. It began to be clear to him that Rachel did not want him to stay.

Hurrying out of the house, he found a path along the bluff through the bayberry bushes. Presently, he looked down on her encampment: a blue towel and the baby's basket in the middle of the long empty beach. Leaving the path, he slid straight down the dune, filling his shoes with sand.

She was lying on her back with her hands clasped on her stomach. Long, gaunt, stone-colored in the clear morning light, she reminded him of the recumbent figures on crusaders' tombs. As his shadow fell over her, she opened her eyes. "Did you find something to eat?" She closed her eyes again without waiting for him to answer.

"As a matter of fact, I couldn't find the bread, or anything else much." He looked down at her defiantly. She was the other side of desire for him, with her knobbed shoulders and her raw working hands. He liked smallness and softness in women, and a ready response.

"I'm sorry," she said. "I meant to go to the store yesterday."

Jake sat down beside her and drew up his knees. The sand was damp from the night's rain and he felt uncomfortable and possibly ludicrous, sitting there in his city clothes. "I wish you'd told me not to come," he said.

"There's plenty of room."

"Maybe, but you don't want me."

"Oh, Jake!" She laughed. "Look, you're welcome to stay. I don't play hostess, that's all."

"I have the feeling I bother you."

"It would take a lot to bother me, right now."

The baby stirred and made a rasping sound. Jake glanced at the bald head, gleaming in the shade of the cot's canopy. "Does he cry every night?"

"No," Rachel said, sitting up and undoing the strap of her bathing suit. "Turn around."

Jake did not understand for a moment, and then he swiveled around in the sand. The baby began to cry and stopped abruptly.

"I don't want you to talk to me about Ann," Rachel said, as though he had already started.

Jake could hear the baby sucking. It was a strong sound, like water running down a drain. "I have no intention of talking about Ann."

"She's my sister and I love her, but I can't take on her problems."

"You might wonder why she's so upset."

"I expect she has a reason."

Jake turned around. "Look, she knew when she married me what it was going to be like." He stopped, staring at Rachel's breast, flattened by the baby's face.

"I know you make your own rules," she said.

Jake flailed around again. "Let's stop talking this way."

"All right."

Her smugness irritated him more than the hostility he thought he sensed behind it. He stood up, careful to keep his back turned to her. "I'm going up to the house, I have some work to do." At the bluff path, he realized she was not going to call him back.

He sat on the porch for the rest of the morning, going over the first two chapters of his novel. There were many changes to be made and his thick-nibbed pen wore holes in the onionskin. Now and then he looked up. Finally, when she did not appear, he began to count, by twenties and then by tens and then by ones; the numbers drummed in his head while he read the manuscript. He had begun to count during the afternoons he had spent on the flowered window seat in the house where he had grown up. There had been twenty red roses in each row on the material, not counting the first and the last roses, which were severed by the seams; he had never been able to decide whether to include those halves in the total he arrived at every afternoon.

At last Rachel came up the path with her paraphernalia. Jake did not look up, although the typed page faded in front of his eyes. As she came closer, he saw, without raising his eyes, the white line at her thigh where her suit had ridden up. "Do you like Dusty Miller?" she asked.

He looked up. She was holding out a small bunch of gray leaves. He touched them; they were sapless, pliable.

Smiling, she took the leaves away and put them in his room. He saw them in the yellow jug when he went up before lunch.

He knew then that he could stay. He had been dreading the trip back, and he looked gratefully at the Dusty Miller. He thought it was the nicest thing his sister-in-law had ever done, and in the course of comparisons, he remembered a girl he had known at college who had brought flowers—daisies, bachelor's buttons—to put beside his double-decker bed.

When he went downstairs, Rachel was fixing sandwiches. She had tied a ruffled apron over her bathing suit, which gave her an oddly coquettish air. Jake wanted to thank her for the Dusty Miller, but she seemed preoccupied.

They ate lunch together almost without speaking. Rachel's whole attention was absorbed in spooning mashed food into the baby. He pushed it out with his tongue and smeared it with both hands on his cheeks; as far as Jake could see, he did not swallow anything. "He certainly enjoys that," he said.

"It feels good, mashed."

"Isn't it because he doesn't have any teeth?"

"I guess that is the reason. Have you tried it?" With a smile that would have been coy in another woman, she held out the tiny tin spoon. Jake opened his mouth and she pushed in a mound, tasteless and soft as butter.

"I don't know," he said, confused, almost embarrassed. "I don't think I like it."

"That's all right," she said.

After lunch, she took the baby upstairs without a word to Jake about the afternoon. She seemed to expect him to work all the time. Presently he went to the stairs and called up, "Can I borrow your car?" She answered faintly, as though from the top of a tower, "Yes, go ahead." He had meant to ask her to join him but then he remembered the baby and its needs. He did not intend to drive that functioning breast along the public highway.

All afternoon, he rode the sandy lanes, skirting the bluff and the ocean. It was the kind of country he liked, dun-colored, flat, unpicturesque, and it reminded him of the cold marshes in France where he had spent two months finishing his first novel. He had always been happiest alone, free even of the demands of a beautiful landscape. Yet as he drove, he could not shake off a peculiar fusty forlornness, a self-pitying ache that seemed at once familiar and reprehensible, and he remembered the dusty roses on the window seat at home. His mother

had not liked to know that he had spent the afternoon waiting
for her, and so when he finally saw her coming, he would run
to his room and pull down an armload of toys. Still she had
often guessed that he had been counting the roses, and when
he sat over his supper, his face reflecting her pallor and annoyance, she would scold, "Stop moping! What's the matter
with you?" Later, when she washed her face, she scrubbed at
that same expression, the desolate look of a woman abandoned
and hopeless, a woman she could not bear.

For the next hour, he drove without thinking. The car fitted
him closely, sweet with the smell of Rachel's things. There
was a can of baby powder on the back seat, and an anonymous
saturated cloth. Jake felt as though he were sitting inside her
skin. He no longer noticed the threatening pastures, lined at
the edge with gray sea and sky.

Driving back, he saw lights shining from the windows. The
house, fully lighted, seemed to sail the dunes, like a great
liner seen far out at sea. He approached it cautiously. Inside
the front door, he smelled roasting beef and realized that for
the first time he was going to be treated like a guest. He
looked into the kitchen, where Rachel was standing beside the
stove. She was wearing a dark dress and her hair was unpinned;
it fell over her shoulders, limp as seaweed and with, Jake
imagined, a brackish smell. "Did you have a good time?" she
asked, glancing around.

"Very nice. I drove . . ." He began to describe it to her,
enbroidering a little.

She was stirring something in a big tin pot. "I'm making
spinach soup," she said, adding hastily, "It's mostly cream and
sherry. And then there's roast beef—" she threw open the oven
door—"and mashed potatoes and peas."

"What happened?"

"Oh, I took a nap this afternoon. I've been tired, with the
baby."

"I thought you didn't like me," he said recklessly.

"Well, in New York . . . But here, you look as though
you're starving."

"Hardly," he said uncomfortably. But he sat down at the table and tucked his napkin in.

All during the meal, she prattled happily and Jake watched her with surprise. She was pretty when she was flushed, and her body, which had looked so stark in a bathing suit, took on a little softness from her dress. She seemed to be flashing at him with her bright pale eyes and her big teeth, set in her mouth like posts. He wondered what she was thinking, what she was planning, and why she had hidden the baby away.

"When do you have to feed the baby again?" he asked.

"Not until morning, if I'm lucky." She was heaping pink ice cream on his plate and as she leaned down, her long hair brushed his face.

He looked up at her and smiled. "Ice cream, too?"

"Yes, and chocolate sauce."

Jake dug a channel for the sauce and reminded himself, quite calmly, that he had never made love to an independent woman. She would be too proud to load him with her feelings; she would remain, always, a little withdrawn. The family life they shared would be more interesting after this—he imagined glancing at her wryly over the Christmas turkey. They would have made a secret pact against the ordinary strenuousness of that life, against the gaping emotions, the endless demands. He stared at her narrow legs as she went to get the coffee and wished she had a little more flesh.

And then she went upstairs without saying a word. Jake thought she might have gone to undress; it would suit her to forgo the preliminaries. Time passed and he resisted the urge to count by scrambling numbers in his head. Finally he realized that she was not coming back. He got up and went out onto the porch.

Even there, he was surrounded by her. A board creaked somewhere, a shade slapped, and he thought he heard a remorseless sucking. He went out onto the grass, preferring the anonymous crepitation of the trees. The dew had fallen and his sneakers were quickly soaked. He tried to believe that she would come to him later and turned over images which he knew did not fit. She would not appear in tears to complain about her husband, she would not lie in langorous positions on the broken rattan couch. It began to be impossible to imagine her coming at all.

At last he knew that she had gone to sleep without him. Cold with resentment, he sat a little longer on the windy porch. He imagined her asleep, snuggling into her pillow, her dry lips parted by the tip of her tongue. At that, his anger drained away as though she had chided him—"Foolish! Foolish!"—as his mother used to chide, with equal pleasure and annoyance, when he plunged into her bed on Sunday mornings.

He walked upstairs on tiptoe and undressed stealthily. The Dusty Miller in the yellow jug amazed him with its false implications and he crushed a leaf between his fingers.

Next morning, he woke earlier than he had in years. Sunlight marked squares on the wall and the curtains, wind-lifted, hung suspended. Rachel was already up; he heard her in the baby's room. After a while, she passed his door and glanced in. "Awake?" she asked, surprised.

He sat up in bed and smiled.

"We're going to the beach. Do you want to come?"

"Yes!"

She shook her head. "What's got into you?" and hurried away before he could reply.

Ten minutes later, he met her on the porch and they went down the bluff path together, the baby swinging in his cot between them. At the beach, Rachel lay down exactly as she had before, her hands folded on her flat stomach. Jake stared at her. She was luminous, as though particles of light clung to the small hairs on her arms and legs. At last he stripped off his shirt and stretched out beside her. The air had been cleared: nothing they said or did would have the usual connotations. The plainness of the situation amazed Jake: here was his arm, here was hers, here were his expectations, clearly labeled, and hers were as recognizable. The solemn rotating demands of his life had moved off and hung in the middle distance, whirring, like planets. Meanwhile the baby dozed in his basket and the morning sun grew warm. Jake had brought a book but he did not open it; he lay touching the baby's basket on one side and Rachel's towel on the other. Far away, he heard the shore birds peeping; their cries merged with the baby's wakening cry. Finally he slept.

When he woke, Rachel was looking at him. "It's almost noon. Don't you have to do some work?"

He sat up, dazed. "I guess I can miss a morning."

"I don't mean to seduce you away from your work," she said seriously. "After all, that's what you came here for."

"I'll get started this afternoon," he promised.

After lunch, he brought his typewriter down to the porch. The wind stirred his papers and whirled them over the railing; Rachel helped him to collect stones. The green and gray stones, sparkling with mica, held his attention on the pages, but when he heard her drive away, he gave up and spent the rest of the afternoon dozing and watching. Returning with a bag of groceries, she glanced at the papers and he thought she could tell from the position of the stones that he had not been working. He wanted to tell her that it did not matter, but he was afraid of destroying the excuse for his visit. Over supper, he talked about his work and she listened, vaguely, yet satisfied as though this was what she expected.

The next morning, he woke at seven and hurried downstairs to have breakfast with her and the baby. Everything they ate seemed predigested: the soft-boiled eggs, the liquid cereal, the white bread full of airy holes. The food slipped down his throat as easily as water and he knew that he, too, would soon be gaining weight. After breakfast, he put on his bathing trunks and followed her down to the beach. Since she did not object or even notice, he wore the trunks all day, even at lunch, spilling jelly and junket on his chest. That night, he put on a shirt and she let down her hair and they sat in the circles of light cast by the wine-bottle lamps. When the wind stirred a branch or when the foghorn moaned, he would go to the screen door; big moths were pasted there, feeling for the light. He too was at the source. From time to time, he had looked forward in his life and imagined the tangled objectives of middle age, but he had never before gone back, into the warm recesses before expectation or disappointment, and he felt as he had felt once a momentary certainty. "Spotted spiders, get thee hence," Rachel sang, rocking the dozing baby on her knee.

During the day, she had seemed either perplexed and silent or animated by a strange false glee, but now, Jake thought, she had settled. She had become what she had been before he arrived: a quiet presence, a floating shadow. Her wavering voice drifted up to him next morning when he lay watching the sunlight on the wall, and later, in the early afternoon, he heard her humming in the silent house. "Dusty was the kiss," she sang, making peanut-butter sandwiches for their snack, "dusty was the silver, dusty was the kiss that she gave the Dusty Miller."

On the fifth day, it grew hot; the sun burned off the haze before eleven and at the beach, Jake turned over on his face. "Shall I do your back?" Rachel asked. It did not seem necessary to answer. Her hands worked across his shoulders, rubbing in the sun-tan lotion, and the touch which should have been merely sexual, seemed instead magical, care-taking, firm. After lunch that day, he watched her nurse the baby.

Milk sprang in a three-pronged fountain from her free breast, sank in drops onto the sand, and disappeared. She did not seem to notice the loss, her head bent over the baby, her shoulders hunched around him. Jake wanted to tell her that he had never imagined such bounty, he wanted to make her raise her face and stare, but he was afraid of arousing her smile. He reached out and caught one warm drop in his palm.

To stay, to catch what came, even to lie in wait, calmly, with the hidden assurance that in time all things would come . . . He stretched himself on the sand like a cat beside a fire.

She was silent, she was withdrawn, the baby took everything, yet he felt her warmth lap over him, in wave after wave, until he was submerged, half drowned in her element.

That afternoon, he heard her sweeping the porch and came to take the broom out of her hands. She was looking tired and he told her to go and lie down, but she did not let go of the broom. "It's just one of my jobs," she said.

"Let me do it." He tried to take the handle but she held it firmly.

"You'll spoil me," she said. "I won't be able to get along without you, and you really ought to leave today or tomorrow."

He stepped back and she began to sweep again, with long strokes which grazed his bare feet.

"I don't want to go," he said.

She laughed. "You've liked it here, haven't you? I didn't expect it."

"Why should I go?"

"David is coming tomorrow."

"Can't we both be here?"

"He doesn't like guests."

"Guests!" he piped shrilly.

She laughed again. "That's what you've become, isn't it? Besides," she added seriously, "Ann will want you back."

"To hell with that!"

"Oh," she said, "you are stubborn, you really are stubborn, aren't you?"

The familiar injustice of her humor stopped his mouth. He knew what to expect if he kept on: the slight, gratified smile, the wheedling cruelty. "What time is the next ferry?" he asked.

"Six o'clock," she told him, surprised.

The rest of the afternoon lay between them like a bar. He knew that in some small way she was regretting his departure, and he sat in his bedroom grimly, waiting for the time. Next door, she was humming as she folded a stack of diapers. He got up once and went as far as his door, but the hall floor rose up against his feet. She passed while he stood there, walking silently, her face set forward like the carving on a prow.

At five-thirty, she went out and started the car. He heard the motor and came down with his suitcase. It seemed the last indignity that she had brought the baby, lying in a roll of cloth on the back seat.

The ferry left at the time when they should have been sitting down to dinner. "You can get something on board," she said as he climbed out of the car. "I won't stay to see you off, I want to get back to feed the baby."

"That child is going to be a monster when he grows up."

"I hope so," she said.

She had laid her hand on the edge of the window and he noticed, as he had at the beginning, that her knuckles were big and red. "Good-by," she said softly, and he understood that now he could kiss her. He stepped back. She started the car and drove rapidly away.

On the ferry, he went to the bow, bracing himself against the salt wind. As the island fell away, tears came to his eyes, and he wiped his nose on his sleeve. "Cold!" a man said, passing. "Better get inside." As Jake turned to obey, he wondered why he was usually given advice and consideration, but nothing substantial, nothing with a taste. He remembered Rachel's bounty painfully. If he could have stayed on, quietly, never asking for more—but he remembered the roses on the window seat and the dusty forlornness of his need. It was a relief to get away from all that. He marched down the stairs to the saloon and looked around for the coffee machine. The paper cup was hot and he nursed it carefully, hoarding its warmth between his hands and putting off the time when he would have to taste it—coffee, only coffee, and thin and bitter at that.

THE VISIT

Although Mr. and Mrs. Clifton had money and lived well, they did not care for traveling and so they seldom made the long trip to New York, even after their only daughter had married and settled there. New York was a strange country, where doormen were often rude and headwaiters supercilious; worse, the Cliftons could never be sure that their daughter would be glad to see them. They had to arm themselves beforehand with humorous home anecdotes and even new clothes, although they were both a little ashamed of that. For this particular visit, Mrs. Clifton had bought a new pair of green shoes.

"As though anyone is going to pay any attention to my feet!" she cried when they were dressing in their hotel room.

Her husband glanced at the shoes, held out at arm's length in an expensive box. "I just hope Lulie won't think we expect something, a three-course lunch or something," he said.

"But we wrote them, 'Act like we aren't coming. Don't plan a thing!' "

Mr. Clifton remained grave. "We are going to take little Johnny to the park, and that is all, Louise," he reminded her. "If they mention a meal, we'll say we're already engaged. I don't want Lulie trapped in that awful kitchen."

"But what if she has planned something?"

"Have you ever known her to plan something?"

"No; but we haven't seen them for such a long time."

"Not since the first weekend in April." He could have told her the number of days.

"Well, they've been very busy this summer." Sometimes it was she who complained about the long intervals between visits, and then it fell to her husband to reply that after all a young couple has preoccupations, commitments which prevent . . .

"Johnny will be two years old in another month," Mrs. Clifton went on. "He'll be grown before I get to know him. I wonder if he's already beyond stuffed animals." She glanced apprehensively at the big red box which she had brought from home."

"You never know, they may have decided stuffed animals are unhygienic."

"I don't believe Lulie cares anything about hygiene. Will you ever forget the baby bottles in the sink with the dirty dishes?"

"That was before they had Soula."

"Oh yes, Soula, dear Soula!" They both took pride in the nursemaid, handpicked at home and sent on; she had brought order into their grandson's life. Even Lulie admitted that now, although in the beginning she had distrusted the arrangement.

In the taxi, Mr. Clifton gave the driver his daughter's address and remembered how it looked written on the front of a thick envelope. His letters to Lulie were frequent and detailed, as though a mass of facts about the weather, the dogs, the Saturday walks and the Sunday municipal concerts could convey the tenderness he could not express with elegance or ease. At one point during the summer, when Lulie's letters had grown so sparse and strange, Mr. Clifton had found himself tempted to line the last page of his own letter with X's, although they reminded him more of his wife's cross-stitch embroidery than of kisses. Yet that letter, like all the others, had ended, Affectionately, your father. Still, as he gave the taxi driver her address, Mr. Clifton suddenly clamped his hands on his knees, as though this time he would be able to give her the kisses, without awkwardness or pain.

Mrs. Clifton had also been stirred by the address. "I wonder if they might be persuaded to move next spring. With Johnny getting old enough to play outside, I should think they'd be a little more uneasy about the neighborhood."

"You know they can't afford to live anywhere else, as long as Larry isn't working."

"Couldn't you increase her allowance?"

"It's all tied up in the trust. I can't do anything about it, you know that." From habit, his irritation with his wife was transformed into a special tone of tenderness and reason, which she recognized and hated: he was absolutely immovable when he spoke so lovingly. Really, she would have liked to ask, "Bob, do you think she's happy?" but she knew the question would bring tears to her eyes. It was a sentimental reflex, left over from her childhood when expressions of affection, no matter how routine, had reduced her to rubble, although she had been fairly well protected against carelessness or spite.

"I wonder if she's put on any weight," she said after a while, approaching the target cautiously from another direction.

"She may have allowed herself a pound or two," Mr. Clifton said gloomily.

"I'll never forget the relief when she finally got thin. Do you remember, it was the summer before she went to college. She came out of it thin as a rail, and we gave her all new clothes for a reward."

Mr. Clifton did not answer. He never discussed the summer day when Lulie had suddenly abandoned the sensible diet and effortless exercises; for he had realized that his daughter had lost her virginity when he came down one morning and found her eating three fried eggs.

He had defended his wife from the discovery, knowing that she would not be able to bear it. Also that morning he had noticed Lulie's neck, set like a stake in the circle of her white collar: he had not wanted to loose the vestiges of her affection, and he had known she would not stand any attempt to control her.

"Of course now she's been pregnant, it doesn't matter so

much; a pound or two might even be becoming." Mrs. Clifton was pursuing her own way. Usually her little system of rewards and punishments seemed charming to her husband— harmless, anyway—but now suddenly he was angry.

"Yes, and I wonder if you remember how she hated being pregnant, how she loathed gaining weight. I always thought that had some connection with the way you tormented her about eating."

Mrs. Clifton stared. "Why, Bob!"

"I'm sorry." He touched her hand. "I guess I'm nervous."

"Well, I don't know why."

They rode the rest of the way in silence, as though anything they said now would reveal too much, upsetting the balance they managed to maintain between the things they guessed at, feared, or imagined and the cheerful observations they offered to each other, lovingly, in good faith.

A few minutes later, they stood on the sidewalk, looking up at their daughter's building. As they had often agreed, it really could be worse looking: a dissected brownstone, its pocked façade was half hidden by a flourishing heaven tree. That there was nothing to be done about the decaying stone— "The landlord says it just keeps falling," Lulie told them— seemed ominous to the Cliftons, who had never encountered anything which could not be repaired with the right skill and outlay of money. Still, there was the tree, and they both looked at it gratefully as they climbed the steep outside stairs.

Mr. Clifton pressed the gummy doorbell next to his daughter's name. After a few minutes, he pressed it again. This time, they heard it, twanging away in the depths of the house. Mr. Clifton peered through the narrow window. The hall inside looked so foreign he wondered if they could have come to the wrong place. "It's strange, I don't see Johnny's stroller," he said incautiously, and heard his wife draw a breath.

Finally he pressed the button again and stepped back in order to avoid hearing the bell drill away inside the empty apartment. His wife had pressed her face against the window too, and, when she turned around, there was a dark smudge on the tip of her nose.

"What are we going to do?" she asked.

"Here, there's a smudge on your nose." He handed her his handkerchief. Having pocketed it again, he said, "You wait here, I'm going down to the drugstore to telephone."

"Don't leave me here by myself," she murmured.

"Now, sweetheart. I'll be back in five minutes. You need to stay in case somebody comes to the door."

"Nobody is going to come," she said. "They've gone away somewhere." There were tears in back of her voice.

"Louise! Probably they're in the back room with the television going. You know how hard it is to hear the doorbell in the back room." As he turned away, she sat down on the step and placed the big red box beside her.

Hurrying down the street, Mr. Clifton repeated his daughter's telephone number to himself, which he had never used; there was something intrusive about a long-distance call—he had never known how it might find her. He went into the shabby drugstore and sealed himself in a booth. He dialed, and then as the telephone began to ring, he felt the emptiness of his daughter's apartment close around him, as though he were lost and she were searching for him, as though the telephone ringing were his own voice peeping, Here I am, here, here, here. He hung up on the sixteenth ring and crept out of the booth, hardly noticing a large woman who was seated at the counter with a stroller parked by her knee.

"Why, Mr. Clifton!"

Even before he turned to her, his confidence was restored. He hurried over, his hands raised in thanksgiving. "Soula! We've been ringing and ringing, up at the house."

"Miss Lulie's out," Soula said, letting herself down off the stool.

Mr. Clifton bent down and kissed his grandson, who was sitting in the stroller eating a chocolate ice-cream cone. The child looked up quietly and continued to lick.

"Say howdo to your grandpappydaddy," Soula ordered. "His

mama had him up till God knows when last night," she explained when the child did not comply. Then she started the stroller briskly toward the door. "Let's go find your granma."

Following in her wake, Mr. Clifton felt almost entirely reassured.

At the end of the street, his wife was still sitting on the step with the red box beside her. Mr. Clifton hurried toward her. "Here they are, Louise!" he called from some distance.

She stood up. "Lulie?"

"She'll be here." He pointed to the stroller. "Just look at Johnny!"

"Good morning, Soula," Mrs. Clifton said with a distracted smile. Then she looked at her grandson. "Sweet lamb," she murmured. "My, he's grown."

"Yes, ma'am, he's a big boy now," Soula said. They all watched the child jam the end of the ice-cream cone into his mouth; chewing, he returned their stares.

"Did Miss Lulie go out this morning?" Mr. Clifton asked after a while.

"Yes, she did. She'll be right back, she just stepped out a minute." Soula laid hold of the stroller and began to drag it up the stairs. Mr. Clifton hurriedly extracted his grandson from the harness and carried him up, gingerly, as though he might press him too hard. Soula fumbled in her pocket for the key.

"Mr. Larry is out too?" Mrs. Clifton asked.

Soula did not answer until they were all in the little dark hall. "Yes, he's out, right at the moment," she said. Then she reached for Johnny. "He's bound to be wringing wet."

Mr. Clifton found himself holding onto the child a moment too long; he felt Soula gently tug one of Johnny's arms. The child turned to her limply.

"We brought something for him," Mrs. Clifton said, holding up the big red box.

Soula smiled. "I'll bring him back soon as I get him changed. You make yourselves at home." She started down the hall, carrying the boy in the crook of her arm. As she dis-

"Has it really been a year," her father said.

"Two years, actually. We haven't had much fun together since Johnny was born."

"Why didn't you tell us before? Then we might have been able to help. Now, there's nothing we can do," her mother said.

"Yes, there is something." Lulie drew herself up, clasping her hands behind her back.

"What is it? Anything . . ." Her father hesitated.

"You can give me some money," Lulie said.

Mr. Clifton plunged his hand into his pocket.

Lulie laughed. "Oh, I don't mean right this minute. I have enough to see me through the day. But I do need my allowance increased."

"Larry will have to give you alimony," her mother said.

"I guess so, if it comes to that. But I need more right now."

Mr. Clifton took his hand out of his pocket and smoothed the flap.

"What do you need it for?" Mrs. Clifton asked.

In the silence, the space between them seemed to take on a new shape. Lulie stared at her mother. "This is the situation," she began in an even voice.

"Larry really ought to be giving you money," her mother murmured.

Lulie stopped.

"Just tell us how much you need," Mr. Clifton said hurriedly.

"Wait a minute," Mrs. Clifton said.

"You disagree?" Lulie asked softly.

"The first thing for you to do is get out of here. Come on home with the baby and get some rest. Then we can sort things out. There's no point in you going on alone here, in squalor."

"Squalor?"

"Your mother is exaggerating to make her point," Mr. Clifton said.

"I don't think going home will help," Lulie muttered.

"You can't go on living alone here, with the baby, in this neighborhood."

appeared, Mr. Clifton gritted his teeth and his wife looked at him with dismay.

"Is something the matter?" she asked softly.

Mr. Clifton turned abruptly and went into the living room. There, at least, nothing had changed. Two uncurtained windows gave onto the heaven tree, and the bare floor was checked with dust and light. The furniture was leggy and sparse; a few good pieces, passed on by the family, stood among the Danish chairs and the rickety tile-topped tables. The room was slightly, stalely disordered; there were papers on the floor by the desk and the sofa cushions were crushed, not as though someone had sat there but as though the sofa were caving in, collapsing from dreariness and disuse.

"Look here, Bob," Mrs. Clifton said from the window.

Lulie's house plants were huddled on the sill. The ivy hung dried out over the edge of the pot and the chrysanthemum had browned from the bottom of each stalk to the bloom. "They haven't been watered for weeks," Mrs. Clifton said. "Weeks! And she always took such pride in them."

"Now, Louise," Mr. Clifton began, and then he stopped and stood staring at the plants, repeating to himself silently the words he had meant to say: such a long summer, such a hot summer, such a hot summer in the city.

"We should have told her to come home in June," his wife said in a low, hurried voice. "We should simply have bought her a ticket and arranged for the baby. We should have insisted. She needed a rest—I knew that! She needed to get away!"

"She wouldn't have been willing to leave Larry alone all summer."

"Well then he could have come too! We would have paid for him. We should have insisted!" Mrs. Clifton cried in her small, cheeping voice. "All her life, Lulie's needed to be told: do this, do that, get some sleep, don't eat too much. Now she's gotten herself into some trouble."

"Hush," Mr. Clifton said, and he went over to the sofa and stood looking down at the crushed pillows.

At the same time, they both heard the front door open, and wheeled toward the sound, their smiles forming slowly.

Louise Abel stopped in the hall and looked at them.

"Lulie!" They stepped toward her, holding out their arms. Their smiles opened wide and fixed. "We've been waiting!"

"I'm sorry," Lulie said. She did not seem surprised.

They reached her at the same moment and their kisses fell lightly and quickly on her cheeks. "Did you forget we were coming? So easy to do," her mother said compassionately.

"Especially at this God-awful hour," Mr. Clifton added.

Lulie brushed passed them and went into the living room. She was wearing blue sneakers and a wrinkled cotton dress and to her father she looked half naked, unequipped. He stared at her, anxiety overcoming his caution. Pale and thin, her fair hair over her shoulders, she was still the princess dwindling in her tower, and he acknowledged her frail charm with enormous relief. After all, she looked as she had ever since she was ten years old, a little pale and worn, perhaps, and tiresomely untidy, but still pretty in a way which suggested hair ribbons and charm bracelets.

"We rang and rang but nobody came to the door; we were half scared to death," Mrs. Clifton began gaily.

"I went down to the drugstore to call and there was Soula and the baby, having their morning ice cream."

"I had to go out," Lulie said. "My appointment is at nine."

Mr. Clifton continued quickly, "I don't know why we said we'd get here so early."

Mrs. Clifton held up the big red box. "We brought Johnny a present."

"Oh!" Lulie said, and took the box from her mother. As they stared, she snapped the string and lifted off the top. "Oh, a bear!" She took the animal out and held it up; its yellow eyes winked in the sunlight. She examined it rapidly, touching the red knitted jacket, stroking the tufted ears, probing the back until she found the squeaker.

EEK EEK EEK EEK

Mr. Clifton took the bear and propped it in an armchai "It's for Johnny," he said.

"What about me? Don't I deserve a present?"

Mr. Clifton's mouth worked; each word had to be chewed out of silence. "Why are you acting this way?"

Lulie sighed. "Do we have to get serious? I guess we do." She took a pack of cigarettes off the table, lit one, and then offered the pack to her father, who waved it away. "Larry left me," she said finally. "Or rather, I left him."

"Oh Lulie—"

"Lulie!"

She turned away and her long hair swung down, hiding her face. Mr. Clifton reached out to touch her and then, daunted by the swaying mass of hair, which seemed electric, menacing, he drew back.

"How long—" His wife gave a little sob and turned away, fumbling blindly in her purse.

Mr. Clifton put his arm around her.

"Actually, he's been gone almost a month," Lulie said. "I made him go. We haven't been living together, really, for a year."

"A year!" Mr. Clifton gasped.

"We've been living in the same house, but that's about all."

Mrs. Clifton blew her nose, folded the handkerchief, and put it back in her purse. "Please tell us what happened."

Lulie stared at the floor. "Nothing happened."

"But you two got on so well, you had so much in common!"

Mr. Clifton intervened. "Wait a minute. In the beginning—"

"In the beginning, it was O.K.," Lulie agreed. "At least we could spend the night together."

Her mother sighed. "I never understood where you got your hardness," she said. "You always could say anything, words never seemed to hurt you. Why is that, Louise?" she asked with wan objectivity. "Why are you so hard? Is it something we did?"

Lulie smiled. "I wouldn't have gotten through this last year without a little hardness."

"Maybe I'll move," Lulie said desperately. "If you can some-how get me some more money. . . ."

"We were talking about that in the taxi coming over," Mrs. Clifton explained. "The trouble is, it's tied up in your trust."

Lulie looked at her father.

"That's right," he said wretchedly. "It is tied up."

"Well, then, I guess I'll have to let Soula go," Lulie said.

"You are not going to do that," her mother said.

"There doesn't seem to be any alternative."

"Johnny is not going to be sacrificed. You know that! His happiness must come first."

"His happiness depends on mine, I guess," Lulie said. She put up her arms suddenly and stretched and her rib cage rose through the thin cotton dress. "I've been thinking about it a long time. I want Johnny back."

Mr. Clifton put his hand on her shoulder. "Lulie. Let me pay for Soula."

Mrs. Clifton said sharply, "You don't know how she'll use the money."

"I'm sure if she tells us—"

"You want to shrug this off, don't you?" Mrs. Clifton asked him. "You've always been like that. When she was little, you never wanted any trouble. 'Call the nurse,' you'd say when she acted up. You've always been glad to spend money sending her places where other people could deal with her—boarding school, camp, college. Plenty of money! But when it came down to doing something about her yourself—oh no! That's too much, that's too demanding."

"I don't want something done about me," Lulie said, "at least not by you."

They did not hear her. Facing each other, they stared for a moment, fixed and still, and then both of them turned their faces away.

Mr. Clifton took his checkbook out of his pocket. "Where is a pen, I need a pen," he said, looking around the room. Lulie brought him one and he wrote the check in midair, his mouth sawing. The writing was very small except for the amount, which was printed in block letters, filling the line. The signature was hardly there at all.

"Here." He tore the check out and put it in Lulie's hand.

Mrs. Clifton said, "Is that all you're going to do?"

"Come on. We're going." He started toward the door, then turned blindly and scooped his wife's coat off the chair.

"Money, always money," she said as he pulled the coat up over her arms.

On the steps, they both turned back. Lulie was standing in the hall, watching them, the folded check in her hand.

"Keep in touch, will you?" Mr. Clifton said.

Lulie nodded. A smile, like a reflection of light, slipped rapidly over her face as she reached out to close the door.

"Oh Lulie!" her mother cried and held out her hands.

The door closed softly.

The heaven tree had scattered a few leaves on the steps and Mr. Clifton took his wife's arm to help her through them. She was sobbing softly and mildly and she continued to sob as they walked together to the corner.

Mr. Clifton looked quickly up and down the street. "I wonder where we'll find a taxi." Then he shook his wife's arm once, lightly, and glanced at her face. "It's over, Louise. Stop crying. We're out in the street." After watching her for another moment, he sighed and reached for his handkerchief. "Here."

"Oh thank you, darling," she muttered, pressing the handkerchief over her eyes. He waited until she had taken it away and then he let go of her arm and stepped out into the street to wave down a taxi.

THE WAY IT IS NOW

I thought my heart broke the last time I saw him, at the final signing. He was being so good, so courteous and kind: "Where, here?"—his pen in his hand. I remembered his gentleness to me, lost during the year when we tore ourselves in two. I came to him out of the slavery of childhood; he signed me into life, but we did not learn from each other.

Then he stood up with his lawyer and I stood up with mine as though we were about to step out and do a figure. I imagined taking his arm, the lawyers hooking up. He looked at me, taking note of the day's orders, given to myself now by myself but still according to his old rules. He liked me to look neat and sly, brazen yet artfully girlish. I stood waiting for his verdict on my new black dress. He smiled. "Black is for funerals." A tiny fleck of viciousness appeared on his lips. Then he swept out, his lawyer behind him.

He could have thanked me, at least, for behaving so badly. I have justified him forever with my lover, my possible neglect of our child. Abused, unenlightened, he will feast on the hearts of our friends, he will seize their sympathies and crack them open, he will be billed and taloned with righteousness: my husband once, now always my judge.

My new hope had promised me an expensive lunch as a reward for the action he claims no part in; I rushed to meet him. The restaurant was dim and I glided to his table, tearful, aqueous in the pale green light. He laid hold of my knee under the red-checked tablecloth.

"How was it?" he asked.

"Oh, good," I said, cherishing his sense of humor. "Aren't you proud of me?"

He nodded and smiled at the little girl, he grasped the grown woman's knee. Presently he would make love to the woman's body to the tune of the girl's shy shrieks. He would like me to continue my double-decker life forever.

But I am trying to vow: not for him, dark to the other's blond, short to his tall. He would place me in the same tight corner, I order a drink, my knee wedged between his fingers. He tells me he has just visited my son and I am furious with jealousy. He is sentimental about him, unloving. I am tormented by my little boy, unable to forget. Now that I sleep alone, he has invaded my bed; urine-soaked, dangling his teddy, he arrives at four in the morning. I am armed with good reasons against him, but every time I hear his forlorn flipflapping feet in the hall, I know I must lay down my life.

"How long is it to Sunday?" my boy asks. Sunday is his father's day.

Or, "You two got young when you got married," leavening my cliché with his own truth.

We are eating steak and Steven has to let go of my knee. One appetite covers the other; he only eats peanuts in bed. I look at his face. Six months of my disturbance have not disturbed him; after our occasional nights together, he reads the paper thoroughly and eats honey with a spoon. I have become one of his luxuries, as essential as the rest.

God, I hate this girl in her black dress, two hundred dollars yesterday and already shabby; she wears her scratches like life wounds. I have felt nothing, suffered nothing, and I will have my revenge for that. The tears I do not shed now will sow dragon's teeth in this man's bed; he will lie on my torpor and toss and complain in silence. Now he supplies me surreptitiously with his handkerchief. I have moved from cotton to linen.

"You have a smut on your nose," he says.

After lunch, we are going to a gallery—this is to be my day of treats—and as we walk along, we stop to look in the beautiful shop windows. One is devoted to props for yachts and we pop in there to buy a skipper-blue ash tray he admires. I remind him that he has no yacht as yet and he replies with glee that his apartment is his castle. I think of that bleak demesne where the iron-skinned philodendron bears its burden of dust. We will go there after the gallery, to have tea and see about more.

Determined to please, he insists on having me try on a snake-skin skirt in the neighborhood boutique. It is so short my thighs are cruelly exposed and when I step out of the fitting room there is so much disappointment in his face I put my hands over my eyes. When I take them down, he is smiling. We carry the skirt away in a yellow bag and I want to apologize to him. It has never occurred to me before that his dreams are brand new.

We are both blind with disappointment by the time we reach the gallery and the paintings sail past us like moons. Only one, a landscape with flowers, forces its way into my eyes. "I wish we could go to the country," I say. The light in the gallery is lunar cold and it is freezing lines into my face.

"That's the first thing you've wanted all day. We'll get my car, it's around the corner."

"I'm afraid your philodendron will miss me."

"It won't but Johnny may."

He goes to call the sitter, seizing the gallery telephone before the lizard it belongs to can object. The lizard glares while Stephen explains that we will be delayed for many hours. I hear my boy crying on the other end and step back to the window so I will not be pierced. Then we march out together, arm in arm, leaving behind us the piny fragrance of quick decisions.

His car is very small and I sit in it coyly, my knees under my chin. He pulls back the canvas top. "Isn't it a little cold for that?" I plead, but he has already opened the glove compartment to get out a woolly scarf. He ties it around my head and makes a great bow under my chin, and I imagine I look like a dog-eared birthday present.

Backing up, shooting out of the slot, he flies at the traffic like a maniac dog. An enormous bus looms, snuffling, behind us. He turns to stare it down but it defeats us with a gassy blast and sails past, rearing its hindside in our faces. "Damn thing!" he shouts and wheels our carriage violently across two lanes. We are going down the cross-town, which will take us to the river. "I want to be out of here in twenty minutes," I say.

He takes me at my word and drives with silent fury. After four blocks, we reach the river, which is gray and flecked with ice. It is mid workaday week and there is no traffic. As the highway hums away, I realize that we are in for the country for sure.

"Johnny was crying when I called," he shouts over the wind.

"I know."

"The sitter said he'd just woken up."

I remember the way he looks when he wakes up, thick with sleep, balancing on the edge of a tantrum. One word and he topples over. "He's always mad when he wakes up," I say.

"I guess it was bad of me to take you away."

"Oh, no. It was bad already. You can't make it worse."

"I hoped a drive would help."

"Don't sound like you've given up." Suddenly I am at it again. Tears do not come out of my eyes; they break out all over my face, like pimples.

He puts his arm around me and pulls me in, close against his side. I feel enclosed or trapped and helplessly comforted. It is warm and snug under his arm. I know with him I will never need to think much or even worry because he is quick and sure and full of energy.

"Where are we going?" I ask; it is an assertion of will.

"Just out to Tarrytown." We have been there before, to picnic in a private place he knows.

It is beginning to snow and the small flakes burn our faces. I am reminded that Christmas is coming and the downslope of the year. It has never seemed probable that I will make it to spring. The road is beginning to ice up. "What a day for an accident," I say.

"That would be fine for me but you are supposed to stay alive for Johnny."

I am fat to his irony; it slices through me with a sizzling sound. "I don't want him to be worse off than I am. That I won't allow. Bad, but not worse off than me."

"He's better than you already. He knows what's going on."

"I know what's going on but what good does that do? I don't know how to stop it."

"You stop it by wanting something else, I guess," he says darkly.

"But I never wanted anything else. The ordinary things seemed like miracles to me: love, food, children. I never believed they could happen to me and when they did, I would have died to keep them. Only they went anyway; not the food."

"I never thought it could happen and so I never tried. Before." He tightens his tweed pressure on my neck and I wonder if I am going to get out of his love alive.

"Why are you trying with me?"

"Because you know what can go wrong."

"But I don't know why."

"Who needs reasons? I need you, warm and whole and working every minute. With him, you were in a daze."

"It wasn't bad, though. He never expected much. Good manners at breakfast, a kind word during the day. I can't remember anything I did that bothered him."

"How nice."

"My parents always said they never quarreled. I didn't know what to call the iron spine between them. Was it pleasantness? I had my hand on it every day but nobody else knew it was there. It's true they never disagreed."

"Better to have a few ugly fights to make you look up and live." It is as close as he will come to making his own excuses.

We have come to the turn-off. There is a slick of ice on the side road and our little car begins to glide dreamily. I look out the window and see the curb coming rather fast. "Hey, watch it!" I shout in a voice I thought I'd lost. He does something manful and contradictory to the steering wheel and we are righted.

"I guess you don't want to die." He is beaming.

I laugh before I notice that he means it, and then I am left with the chopped-off laugh hanging out of my mouth like a piece of spaghetti.

We are still a long way from the private place, but he swerves off the road. It is the entrance to a religious institution, an old estate, with rhododendrons marching up the drive. There is a large sign warning against trespassing, but he stops the car and jumps out to jerk the top up. His white breath bursts above my head and his hair shines with snow. It is the first time I have looked at him in a long while and I realize with surprise that he is very handsome. He clamps the roof down over me and climbs in, and we spend a few minutes settling ourselves and getting the heater started. Then there we are, sealed, with the windows beginning to fog up.

I wonder if I will get back in time to bathe Johnny.

He reaches out and I do not see how it can still be so fresh and awkward. Then he pulls me up against his jacket and I lie inert, my nose an inch from his pale soft neck. This lovely quiet inertia may be love. When I first felt it, it was a revelation, a star in the East, but now I am not so sure. Torpor and resignation feel like love to me: the grooves are all the same.

"You never talk seriously," he says. "Even today, I have to sit and listen to your jokes."

"Well, I'm sick of crying. Tears ruin my complexion."

"I want your hard heart," he says, pressing. "You see, I can't get out of your lingo."

"I wonder why I am so communicable. He caught it right away. He got to be so glib and smart, and the best thing you could have said about him at the beginning was that he was sentimental. Now Johnny is starting to sass that way."

"Stop drifting."

"I'm not drifting. They're all right here."

"Well, they won't always be," he says with desperation. "Six months or a year and you'll have some perspective on this. Then I want you to marry me."

It takes me a while to choke that down. "I thought we agreed to let things slide."

"I wanted you to get through the legalities on your own, so you'd know it was your own doing. But once that's all over, I want a chance. I love you, Ann."

I have never been able to believe plain speaking; it sounds mechanical to me, chattery, like the words those strange dolls speak who have a string in the middle of their backs. Now it makes me angry. He ought to know by now I can't believe. It is important to say something to spite him. "I know it's ridiculous, Stephen, but I can't remember what color your eyes are."

"What?" His arm loosens a little.

"I know they're not brown. I must have looked a thousand times! But are they gray or blue?"

"Don't start these games, Ann."

I hate the way he repeats my name, hammering it like a nail. "Let's go back to town," I say, and wish I were equal to issuing a command.

"You haven't answered me."

"Oh yes I have."

"I know you don't want to hurry into something."

"It isn't that. Time won't make any difference. It's the way I've been gouged out. There's nothing in me you'd want; I have to be left alone."

"I'm not sure you can manage, alone."

"At least the same things won't start happening again."

His face intervenes between my eyes and the windshield. "Then why don't you tell me no?"

He is smarter than I expected; he knows my rotten spot. I can find all the reasons, but the final no is not in my power. I am afraid of being left alone. Other people get to the ends of things and feel relieved; the pressure is off, there is peace at last. But I hate even getting to the end of pain; at least when I hurt I know I'm living.

"Is it yes or no?" he insists.

I try to rage a little. "You want me to say yes and pretend I don't know what that means. Another good beginning. All the habits loosened: screwing in the middle of the afternoon when Johnny is in the park and holding hands in the movies and saving the mail for each other. How long would you say it might last?"

"A while. Long enough."

"And then it would start happening again. There's something left out of me—energy, hope. The first disappointment would be my last. I won't keep on trying."

"I'm different from him."

"Maybe. I don't know. I'm blind and deaf to you half the time and the other half I see what any moronic schoolgirl would notice on the bus: a good-looking man."

"That sounds O.K."

I won't stop for his smile. "They say people learn. I haven't learned. The little lines in my brain are still the same. Get me started on the marriage track and I'll toddle along, pleased as punch till the first bad time. Then I start slowing down. Before you know it, there's a dead stop. I'd scare you by not eating but it wouldn't be because I wanted to starve. I'd just want to stop, rest, be left alone."

"All right. I'll leave you alone."

I am still talking while he starts the car and backs out of the drive. I am still talking on the side road and on the highway, raising my voice above the wind. I want him to go on watching and listening, never quite despairing. After ten miles the words are gone and I sit silent, staring at my gloves, which are dirty and worn.

We are racing back to town in a fireball of silent rage. It is already dark and the snow is falling through the spears of our headlights. At least we are still joined by the car, our shared metal skin. A truck piles past us, its running board level with my shoulders, and I wonder about quick death together, the sentimental end. But I know he will go on forever; there are other ways for him, certain satisfactions. At the cross-town, I begin to smell my apartment: hamburgers and scorched coffee and a sour baby undershirt stiffening on the radiator. Those three rooms hold me, head, hands, and feet. Johnny will be waiting for me but he will scream when he sees me, then ask for a present and fall on the floor when I say I have nothing for him.

Stephen stops, double-parked for a fleeting second in front of my door.

I am somehow still talking.

"Listen, I was trying to say—"

"You don't want to try again."

"I never tried in the first place!"

"Good night, Ann." He reaches across me to open my door and I snatch his arm.

"Come up and have a drink?"

He looks at me as coldly as he can. "I don't see the point."

"For old times' sake." I am holding his arm tightly, knowing he will not jerk it away.

"Old times are over."

"New times, then." It doesn't matter what I say; I am feeling for words and watching his face to see which one will hook him. It's done: he turns to open his door.

"All right," he says. "For a few minutes."

As I crawl out of the car, cross the sidewalk, and begin to fumble for my key, I hear the organ bleats which summoned my first husband to our undoing. I need you, I need you, I need you. Already my relief is gone and I feel the grid bars of consequences across my face. We look at each other through this grill and I smile to make it better.

"They're brown, or maybe hazel," he says, taking the key out of my hand.

THE OLD WOMAN

At five o'clock, the two sisters, Eustace and Lily, heard the car and went to the living-room window. They had been waiting all afternoon, talking and looking at magazines, and as they leaned out of the window, their faces were already set in ironic smiles. Below them, the green sports car plunged around the circular drive and stopped a few inches from the column of the porte-cochere. There was a pause, and then the car door was opened and their mother lurched out. Her hat flapped on her back and her large black purse gaped open; she looked as though she had been hurled. As soon as she was out, the door closed smartly and the car backed up, churning gravel, and dashed off, its rear window flashing. Neither of the sisters had caught sight of the couple inside.

Clucking and giggling, they ran down the stairs. "Mama!" they cried, their voices imitating the real cries of distress which had rung through their childhood. "Mama!" She had sunk down in a heap on the porch steps. As they gathered her up, each taking an elbow, they felt for the first time her full weight, which would be theirs from now on to support until they handed her tenderly into the grave; she indicated as much with a flip of her hand. She had grown accusingly old during the course of the afternoon; her lips blabbered, her powdered jowls shook, and only her blue eyes, blue as the wing stripe of a female mallard, remained unchanged. She jolted up the steps between her daughters, her toes knocking the rungs. At the front door, she stopped and looked up at the fanlight, where her dead husband's initials were embedded in the glass. Her eyes suddenly streamed tears. "Pig!" she hissed.

Eustace spread her out carefully on the living-room sofa. "You shouldn't have gone with them," she remarked. "You knew perfectly well they wanted to be by themselves."

"Oh, pig!" the old woman gasped. "I gave him that car myself!"

Lily wrenched off one of her mother's high-heeled shoes. "Indian giver. You're always taking back."

The old woman jerked her foot out of Lily's hand. "Leave me alone, leave me in peace," she whimpered, punching the sofa pillow and laying her face in the dent.

Lily went to the door at once, but Eustace lingered. Softer and blonder than her sister, Eustace was already running to sweet fat and sentimentality. She said, "He's crazy about that girl, you know that, Mother. You should have had more sense than to butt in."

"They asked me to go with them," the old woman said with dignity.

"They had to ask you, the way you were acting."

"Little chit with no pants on. I saw when she got in the car."

"That couldn't be true, Mother," Eustace said with some heat. "They're being so good. Tony told me himself, volunteered it, that they've decided to wait."

"Huh!" the mother snorted.

"Come along, Eustace, she only wants to prolong it," Lily said.

At that the old woman moaned, "I'm killed!" and began to sob. Her sobs were cut off by the sound of the living-room door closing. She sat up and stared. They had gone: she could hear their footsteps on the stairs. Gasping at their heartlessness, she snatched off her hat and sailed it like a platter across the room.

Then she sank back, clasping her breast. Oh, to be able to die, killed on the spot! Her own mother had died of a heart attack in the middle of a family scene. But nothing would kill her; she would outlive them all and bear the blame for their rotted lives and early deaths. She lay with her hand on her breast, feeling for a preliminary throb. The window shutters had been closed in the heat of the day and the room was dusky and close; late sunlight barred the walls, crossing the faces of her husband, her daughters, and her only son which hung on green velvet ribbons over her desk. To have them all dead and gone, crossed out, to live her last years free of the squalor of their needs and affections! She had lived in an emotional piggery since she had first stepped into this room, a bride, but already pregnant and bilious with regret. The years had not reconciled her to this room—her room—with its stripped pine paneling and pale green paint; the faces and facts of her children leaned out from the walls and lurked in very niche and drawer. Their lives overflowed and submerged her even now. The girls hated her, yet they came with hateful regularity to eat at her table, to dine on her vitality. Thin-blooded creatures with no passions of their own, they came to feed on her energy as they fed on her country ham and smoked turkey. Only her youngest, her son, her hope for love, had set his teeth against her.

He was the only one whose childhood she remembered, out of her twenty years of raising. He had been separate from the beginning. She had even had to struggle to feed him; he had bitten her nipple, nursing, and later fringed the edge of his silver spoon. She had forced food into him, as later she had forced his schooling into his brain. Finally, he had subsided, becoming quick and silent, going his way, which seemed to run parallel to her wishes. They said he was like his father. She knew nothing about that. His father had dropped out of her life somewhere in the web of birth and raising; he had slipped easily enough through the strands. She had hardly missed him until they sent word that he was dead, and then she had been angry at him for going away to strangers when she might, at least in the end, have loved and nursed him. She had loved and nursed Tony, in spite of his rebelliousness; mothering him, she had felt the return of her own young life, the long-delayed comeback of her hopes.

And now he had turned against her, expelling her even out of his silence, because of the girl! All she wanted was for them both to love her. Tears rose in her eyes again. Well, it was too late for that: the little chit was set against her, with her sharp jaw and her flat blue eyes, the wrong blue, too light, too fey. Too late for that. Too late. Never too late! She would not allow it! And so she had insisted in her pig-headedness that she would ride with them in the motor car, depending on her ironic charm to win them over. But they had been impervious, stone-set against her irony as well as her charm. Sitting alone in the back seat, she had hurled her remarks and her laugher at the crowns of their heads. They had not even turned around.

She sat up, swinging her legs down, and admired, in passing, her tiny, unmarked bare feet. Then she padded to the door and threw it open. "Eustace! Get the box!" she yelled up the stairs.

Eustace came to the stair rail. Oh, that big plain girl, plain in her baby ruffles, plain in her little-girl pink, plainest of all in the stiff white linen of her sensible marriage! "Which box?" she asked.

"The present box, you know perfectly well what I mean." She went back to the couch and sat down to wait.

So Tony would love the girl and marry her, half for spite. What did it matter? A year and a baby, and she would become, for him, a solid mass of excuses. Sick, tired, or pregnant, menstruating or suicidal, she would lie like a log across the current of his life. He was only twenty-one, not out of college yet, and possessed of enough meanness to force the world. It would kill her to see him dammed up! but once he had married the girl, he would defend her, and his best energies would be devoted to that. Two years and another baby, and at twenty-three, they would both be stale and reasonable, with small expectations. That she could bear for the girls, but not for Tony. No—she would not stand for it. Let him bring the girl here, to his mother's house. She would provide the room and the bed, she would even bestow her blessing on their lovemaking;

but there would be no marriage. He loved the girl for the exercise of his principles and he would never marry her if his principles were betrayed. He had been wan all summer with abstinence and resolution. "Eustace!" she yelled again.

Eustace came in, red-faced from carrying the enormous box.

"Put it here." The old woman indicated the table in front of her.

Eustace laid down the box. "What are you up to now, Mama?"

The old woman slipped off the top and plunged her hands into tissue paper. Underneath, there were bolts of African cotton sent by a missionary uncle, carved ivory elephants, small jade figurines, envelopes of uncut stones, and some Eastern silks. Everything that wandering relatives had brought back over the years was stored in the box: not worth using but good enough to give away.

"I have something here for that girl," she said, taking out a length of flowered silk.

Eustace fingered it. "It is pretty. She could have made it up."

"I'll make it up for her, myself."

"Better let her find someone to do it, Mother."

"She won't find anyone to do it as well as I can. You know that. I made all your clothes, till you got too fat to bother with."

"You do beautiful work," the big girl said sadly, "but she'll want it done her own way."

"Not when she sees what I can do for her. Half her problem is she doesn't know how to dress."

"I thought you didn't like her," Eustace said.

"Oh, I'll help where I can."

"Tony won't like it. It'll take a dozen fittings, if I know you."

"Tony is going back to college tomorrow."

"Well," Eustace said with pale irony, "he couldn't leave her in better hands."

"Get my tape measure," the old woman said, ignoring her.

Eustace went out. While she was gone, her mother shook out the silk and began to measure it, stretching it from her cheek to her hand. It was Lily who came back finally with the tape measure.

"I don't need it any more," her mother said. "Let me just see how this drapes." She flung the silk over Lily's peaked shoulder and it hung down, shimmering, almost to the floor. Lily stood stiffly under the cool fall of silk. "That girl is taller than I am," she said.

"It's not a prize fight," her mother muttered as though her mouth were already full of pins. "Lined with pale pink silk, I think. And self-covered buttons. Or should I use those little frogs, in pink?"

"It's a bad idea, the whole thing. What did they tell you in the car, to get you so stirred up?"

"They told me nothing!" the old woman suddenly bellowed. "They did nothing! They sat there like stones! And that is the literal truth. They think I disapprove of them."

"But you do," Lily insisted.

"Only of their marrying."

"What else is there?"

"A great deal, as you perfectly well know." The old woman pulled the silk away. Lily had a room of her own, in town, near her office, and was known to be free. "Now where is that girl's telephone number?"

"I don't know," Lily said. "You'd do better to leave her alone."

However, a few minutes later, the two girls were hanging over the stairs to hear their mother's loud trill on the telephone. "Then tomorrow will be all right? Plan to stay to lunch, this is going to take some time." She hung up on the girl's small reply and went into the living room to open the shutters. The sisters heard them crashing against the wall and sighed. Their mother was on her way.

Next morning, the old upstairs nursery was converted into a sewing room. Since there were no grandchildren, and never

would be any according to the old woman's shrewd guess—for
Eustace and Peter had already been married five years, and
Peter was looking more parched every day—the nursery had
never been done over: pale blue Alices still hung on the pale
blue walls. It had not been the old woman's territory and bore,
instead, the marks of several civilizing English governesses.
There was even a dressing gown with a hood on a hook behind the door. Peter had been summoned to sweep these remains away and to carry the old woman's sewing machine from
her bedroom. Bent under the weight of the machine, he
snapped, after an hour's silence: "Why does this have to be
done? You never used to sew in here." His mother-in-law gave
him one of her sweet smiles and he went off to his office in a
sweat.

The old woman walked out herself to buy a small revolving
pedestal with a hem-marker, which she placed in front of the
cloudy pier glass. The linoleum floor was covered by a snow-
white sheet, and Eustace, who had decided to humor her
mother, brought up some of her nasturtiums in a vase.

By eleven o'clock, the room looked so bright that Sylvia
hesitated on the threshold. Tony had left her at the foot of the
stairs, saying, "Call me if you need anything," and she had gone
up automatically, although they had both decided that she
did not want the dress. Tony had said, and she had agreed,
that it was up to her to decline his mother's kindness.

"Come in. We must get started, if we're going to have anything accomplished by lunch," the old woman said. She was
already seated at the sewing machine, and she looked up
brightly at Sylvia. "My, how dressed up you are! Is that in my
honor? I've never seen you wear stockings before. But then,
I've hardly seen you wear anything before." She bent to thread
the sewing-machine needle.

The girl was snapping and unsnapping the clip of her straw
purse. "I want to tell you how much I appreciate it," she said.
"But I really can't put you to all this trouble."

"No trouble at all," the old woman said evenly.

"But it's bound to be, in this heat."

"There is so little I can do for you, let me do this, at least," the old woman said.

"Really, it's too much—"

"Don't refuse me, Sylvia. At my age, there is so little."

The girl stood staring, rebuked. She did not understand how Tony could have left her to deal with this alone.

After a moment, the old woman looked up again, "Why, take off your clothes!" she cried gaily. "I can't fit you in all that."

As Sylvia reached for her back buttons, the old woman sprang up to help. She loosed each button carefully from its hole. Then, turning back the edges, she said with relief, "What a pretty back!" The girl hunched her shoulders. The skin was tanned and smooth, and when the old woman laid her hand on the shoulder blade, she could feel the tiny vibration of Sylvia's heart. "Skin the cat," she said, and pulled the dress off over Sylvia's head. "There, I mussed your hair."

"It doesn't matter," Sylvia said, but the old woman was already ferreting in a drawer for a comb. "I never bother much with my hair, anyway."

"That's a shame. It's such beautiful hair," the old woman said, picking up a heavy strand and darting in the comb. She ran the comb down swiftly, catching snarls, which at first made Sylvia wince; then Sylvia stiffened her neck and stood at attention while each snarl was combed out. After a moment, the old woman said, "Much better," and stood back to admire.

The girl touched her hair tentatively. In her white cotton slip, she looked very young and slight; the shoulder straps were grimy and the little cups on the bodice were only half filled. "I didn't know what underclothes to wear," she said, after a moment during which the old woman stood still hazily admiring. "I mean, is it going to be an evening dress?"

"You might call it that. How thin you are!" The old woman reached out and there was a snap against the girl's thigh. "Oh, you mustn't wear a girdle."

"I always do, in the evening," Sylvia said stiffly.

"Well, this isn't night. Take it off. It'll spoil the lines of the dress." She stood back, arms akimbo. "Besides, men don't like those things."

The girl hesitated, glancing at the door. Tony should have come by now to look for her. She was chilly suddenly, and gooseflesh rose on her long pale arms.

"Go ahead, my back is turned," the old woman said and went to look out the window.

"All right," the girl said, in a little. Turning, the old woman saw her standing sag-shouldered in her white slip, a rubber girdle dangling like a down flag from her hand. Her elbows and wristbones, her knees and ankles stood out sharply. A plucked bird, the old woman thought. She bustled to her with an armload of silk.

As she slung the material over the girl's shoulder, light caught the folds and slid along them and the small pink-and-red flowers winked. The girl gasped at the cool touch of the silk. "Oh, it's lovely!"

"We've just begun," the old woman warned, gathering in the folds. "You must have patience if we're going to make a dress worthy of the material. I never use a pattern; I want my own effect. A wide band here, a cummerbund, to show off your pretty little waist, and then some gathering here—" tactfully, she draped the shrinking breasts—"and then cut to here in back! I always think backs are very attractive. Of course, this is only an approximation." She beckoned the girl onto the little pedestal in front of the mirror. "See!" she said, grasping the material firmly at Sylvia's waist. "See, how pretty!" The girl looked at herself in the mirror and smiled.

Tony came to the door. He would not come in, and Sylvia did not plead with him. He leaned against the doorjamb, his face in shadow. "It is pretty, isn't it?" Sylvia asked; she wanted him to understand that she had mastered the situation.

"That's for you to decide," Tony said abruptly and went back downstairs.

"This summer has been hard on him in ways you may not understand," the mother said apologetically. "Girls have no idea of the strain."

An hour later, when Annie pounded the lunch gong, the two women went downstairs. Tony was waiting in the hall, and he heard them talking as they came down. As soon as Sylvia stepped off the bottom stair, he took her arm. "I thought Sylvia was staying to lunch," his mother said.

"Well, she's not," Tony said, propelling her to the door.

"Good-by," the girl said, looking back.

"Tomorrow at ten," the old woman told her calmly and went into the dining room. "Take these places away," she told Annie as she sat down.

She was still at the table when Tony came back, an hour later. "Come here, please," she called.

He stopped in the doorway. "Mother, I've got to pack and go to the airport."

"I like your girl."

"You don't know her."

"Well, I learned a lot this morning," the old woman said humbly. "You're going to miss her, at college."

"You don't know her," the boy repeated. "I'll call you in a few days."

"Good-by." She held her cheek up for a kiss. When she heard him running up the stairs, she began to roll her napkin between her hands, more and more tightly; after a while, she heard him come down and leave the house. She did not call to him this time, and in a few minutes, she heard the car leaving the driveway. Then she stood up and went to the sewing room to look at the pieces of silk.

With Tony gone, the house became very still. During the week, Lily worked in town, and Eustace was always occupied with waxing, scrubbing, and polishing her hideous development house. Now and then the telephone rang, blooming in the silence of the old woman's room. Sometimes she let it ring, enjoying its importunity more than the requests or demands she would have received if she had answered it. But when the telephone rang four times and stopped, she would go at once to call Tony. Then they would have one of their short, factual talks; neither of them ever mentioned Sylvia. He was working, he was always working, he was working harder and harder, and to the old woman, he seemed to be spinning in a void; she could not imagine how his days passed.

Often the old woman never dressed at all, padding around the house all day in her flannel nightgown, to Annie's silent chagrin: but on Wednesdays, she was always dressed by ten o'clock. That was Sylvia's day to be fitted. From the top of the stairs, the old woman would call to her, "Come up quickly!" and then they would go together into the sewing room. Everything they needed for the morning was arranged on the long table. The silk lay cut like petals, overlapping, and the pier glass gleamed in front of the little pedestal whose top was smudged now from Sylvia's bare feet. "You should wash for Tony," the old woman had said gravely when she first saw Sylvia's feet. "Or does he like you dirty?" The girl had replied, equally gravely, "He's never seen my feet."

Sylvia began to talk, as the days passed, at first only about her family: cornflakes people, she called them, who were afraid of knowing too much. They assumed that she and Tony were fixed together in some permanent way and laid down the burden of their responsibility forthwith. "Why, I could stay out all night!" the girl cried, aggrieved.

"Then why does Tony always come home so early?"

The girl hesitated. "He doesn't want things to . . . go to pieces."

"I believe he's a little frightened," the mother said kindly, pinning in a sleeve. "There. I've scratched you. These silk pins are so sharp."

The girl touched her arm vaguely. "I don't believe he's frightened," she said. "He wants everything to be right."

"That's up to you, isn't it," the old woman said, turning back to the sewing table.

"But I don't know much. And then"—it came throbbing up, out of her transparent reserve—"there's never any privacy."

"You can always come here."

There was a long silence. Leaning down, the old woman touched a handle and swung the pedestal around so that the girl was facing the mirror. "There. What do you think about the length?"

The girl searched for the old woman's eyes in the mirror. "I don't think you understand," she said. In contrast to the heavily flowered silk, her faced looked almost featureless; eyes, nose, and mouth barely marked on the flat unlandscaped pallor of her skin.

"I understand how hard it is," the old woman said, turning the pedestal so that the girl faced her. "Now I want to pin in the zipper." She held it up, sinuous as a little snake.

"Oh, we'll manage all right," the girl said, holding up her arms so that the zipper could be applied.

"Not without knowing each other."

They said no more that day. The fitting was not over until almost one o'clock, and so Sylvia stayed to lunch. They sat facing each other across the long table while Annie shuffled in with plate after plate of food: a secret feast, away in the silent house. Afterward, Sylvia called Tony in Cambridge, and from her room, the old woman listened to the girl's voice and did not need to distinguish the words.

He was coming home for Thanksgiving, and the dress was to be finished before then. By early November, it was already done. The old woman, however, occupied herself with minute changes: the button holes were cut again and reworked, the hem was decorated with lace, and finally Sylvia's initials were embroidered inside a sleeve. The silk was stiff with details; it seemed to stand in the corner of the sewing room.

The warm weather broke before Thanksgiving and a hard frost set in, bruising the last chrysanthemums in the garden behind the house. The old woman arranged nuts and fruits on the dining-room table and the summer cretonne slip covers were finally put away. With lighted fires and velvet hangings, the house seemed rich and strange. Sylvia saw its grandeur and was frightened. The people were not worthy of the house, as she, herself, was not worthy of the elaborate flowered dress. She looked more and more childlike in it, as it approached the final stages, as though her body was being reduced to a framework for the display of the old woman's handiwork. Yet she had never seen such a beautiful dress; and it was cut low in back, down to her waist.

The fire was already lit in the living room on the evening when Tony came home, and the decanters and glasses had been laid out. His mother had gone upstairs, saying that she was exhausted, and Sylvia was left to watch in the hall. Tony frowned when he saw her.

"Oh, Tony!" She put her arms around his neck. In her room upstairs, the old woman listened to the rapid exchange of their voices and heard her son's irritation smooth a little. They went into the living room together, and she could hear no more. Well, she had done her best. Everything was arranged. Only the final leap, the surge of warmth and imagination, she could not provide for them. She sat on her chaise longue, covered to the chin by a thin cotton blanket. They would be sitting down by the fire, sipping sherry—she hoped. She felt it was a good sign that Tony had not yet brought his suitcases upstairs. Perhaps Sylvia was going to be able to persuade him. Then they would have their short blooming and their long painless withering and by summer, it would be over; by summer, they would soar out of this preoccupation—for she had grown fond of Sylvia; she wanted the same liberation for her— and depart, without regrets, on the course of their lives. If only Tony had enough nerve to begin! She had always noticed in him the strength of will, the brutal determination to have his own way, which was so much more powerful than carnal blandishments. He would want his own way especially when it was sterile and bitter; the accomplishment lay in clinging to the original design. A puritan, but only when it went against the grain. And then, the girl was not strong! A few days before, when they had tried on the dress for the last time, the old woman had had to take in a seam; she went on losing weight, poor girl, as though her life were seeping out. There wasn't much there, to offer. Well, she had done her best. Now she sat back, under her thin blanket in the chill room, and looked forward to seven o'clock, when she could go downstairs and ask her son for a glass of sherry.

When she went down, they were sitting by the fire in silence. Tony stood up when he saw his mother. One side of his face was hot from the fire, and she put up her hand to feel the warmth. She might have cried out, My son, My son, if she herself would not have been the first to laugh. She did say that she was glad to see him.

All the delights of his childhood had been prepared for dinner, and therefore it was a curious meal. Shrimp cocktail had been valued, when he was ten, for its sauce, and so the shrimp still lay submerged under a sea of red; the main course was also largely red, although they had always called it Pink Bunny. A chicken hash was the single concession to adult appetite, and Tony refused it almost with indignation and asked if there were no corncakes and syrup. Annie rushed in with the platter and the little silver pitcher. The old woman had been afraid that he might have outgrown his penchants, and she watched him wolf the pancakes with delight. In many ways, he was still unchanged, unsmoothed. She felt that his brilliance lay in his childishness; grown, he would be like everyone else. She wondered if he still had his garish dreams.

"Do you still have those dreams?" she asked when they were eating their chocolate ice cream.

"They're worse than ever," he said with some pride.

"Worse than those murders when you used to wake me up, screaming?"

"Yes. More detailed. More vivid. When I was little, the means were not very clear; now it's all there, every blow, every stroke of the hatchet." He looked across at Sylvia, who smiled wanly. "I'm even allowed to dream about girls."

The old woman had never seen him so gay. He seemed even to have overcome his reluctance, to answer questions. She prodded him a little further. "Do you dream about murdering girls?" But at that he laughed.

After dinner, the old woman went up with Sylvia, to help

her to dress. All the lights were on in the sewing room, and when she took the dress out, the flowers seemed to rise from the silk. She dropped the dress over the girl's bowed head; Sylvia seemed oddly subdued. "You don't have to wear it, you know," the old woman said, in an excess of confidence. The girl hesitated. "But I'll never have such a beautiful dress again!" In the end, the old woman was even able to persuade her to wear two soft little cotton pads to prop up her breasts. The girl was not beautiful, when it was all done, but she was set off with imagination and tact; the meagerness of her body was veiled and attention was drawn to her long smooth back. She looked as though she had a loving mother.

On the stairs, the old woman said in a voice that Tony would hear, "The little room at the end of the hall is ready for you when you come back. I've called your mother. She doesn't want you to drive home on these icy roads." Then she stopped on the landing and let the girl continue alone.

Tony came out of the living room to meet her. He hesitated when he saw her, shining dimly in the light at the foot of the stairs. She held her skirt out with both hands. "Pretty?" she asked. With one step, he was at her side and had her hand on his arm. They went out quickly, without saying good night.

The old woman went to bed at eleven o'clock, after a glass of milk. She lay awake for a few minutes, watching the rays of light from passing cars which shifted across her ceiling. Sometimes when she lay alone at night in the big bed, her life seemed very small; she could have held it, all sixty years of it, in the palm of her hand. Tonight, she felt, instead, the expansion of her hope, as though her life had put out a new branch. Tony was going free—free of love, free of the world. He would carry her own life a little farther.

She was wakened in the morning by the grinding of the wooden shutters as Annie cranked them open. She sat up. "They're still asleep, both of them," Annie said. Then she brought in the breakfast tray.

"Why, you've made me a butter curl," the old woman exclaimed; it was a trick Annie had never been able to learn.

"I did everything I could," Annie said solemnly. Then she bustled out, her lean frame quick with responsibility. The old woman got up and put on her dressing gown.

In tying the sash, she decided to go and see them. She had often visited Tony before he was awake, and she knew that the sound of the door opening never disturbed him: the girl, however, might be a light sleeper. It was a risk worth taking. The old woman hurried down the hall, her bare feet skimming the floor; she felt herself lifted, exulted by expectation and even her shadow seemed to leap behind her. She had not had such a strong sense of herself, of the grainy wooden floor, the touch of her flannel gown, the blazing streams of morning sun—no, not for many years. The doorknob felt warm under her hand.

She turned it slowly and the door opened without a sound. She heard the windowshade flap and felt a current of cold air across her face; Tony had not forgotten to open the window. They were lying on the bed, side by side, and her first impulse was to cover them; she saw their bare feet, and their shoes lined up at the foot of the bed. They were wearing all their other clothes.

She closed the door. For a minute, she stood cursing their lack of feeling, their vapid thin-blooded propriety; but that did not go far enough. She had expected to see such a change, such a startling springing up of life; and to see them instead lying as still as sticks made her feel that nothing was ever going to change for her again. For the first time in years, she remembered her husband's face when she had first met him, and how the change in his expression had made her feel that her life was beginning. And now it is ending, she thought, remembering the children's quiet faces. She leaned against the wall to feel this final pang, and heard instead the rattle of pans in the kitchen as Annie washed up. The day was only beginning—only beginning! And there would be many more days before she could begin to expect the end.